STREET

Also by Jack Cady

The Well
The Jonah Watch
McDowell's Ghost
Singleton
The Man Who Could Make Things Vanish
The Burning and Other Stories
Tattoo and Other Stories
The Sons of Noah and Other Stories
Inagehi

STREET

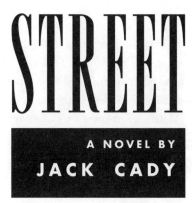

A NOVEL BY
JACK CADY

ST. MARTIN'S PRESS
NEW YORK

Design by Junie Lee

Library of Congress Cataloging-in-Publication Data
Cady, Jack
        Street / Jack Cady.
            p. cm.
        ISBN 0–312–11455–9
        I. Title.
    PS3553.A315S77   1994
    813'.54—dc20   94-13087
                                                                  CIP

ISBN 0-312-11455-9

10 9 8 7 6 5 4 3 2

Dedicated to Seattle's street people, of whom some
served as models for this book.

There is an accursed thing in the midst of thee, O Israel; thou canst not stand before thine enemies, until ye take away the accursed thing from among you.

Joshua 7:13

STREET

I
CHORUS

I am a familiar of shadows, a keeper of sacred flame. Neon and glitter I watch; also plastic, enamel, anodized aluminum on the shiny sides of modern architecture, and the unfogginess of thermopane. I watch from shadows lying in the nave of The Sanctuary, or through stained-glass arches. The Sanctuary is an abandoned church standing in a poor neighborhood of this northwest city. Its belltower rises above traffic like a gray remonstrance. I discovered it long ago, on a green and golden morning during spring.

I walked with a friend that Sunday morning. What took us to this part of town now lies beyond memory. We were actors, and were poor. Perhaps we had been traveling. Perhaps we came from the grafitti and stench of a bus station. We were in love. I certainly remember that. Maybe youth and love were fit reasons to walk. We turned a corner and saw gray walls of The Sanctuary rising almost whitely into sunlight. A spot of brilliant green seemed an ornamental pendent below the dark shadow of nave. A woman sat quietly as we approached.

1

"Look," my friend whispered, "she's gorgeous. A transvestite in the sun."

"I care for no woman but you," I told her, and it was a poor joke.

The woman—he—she—at any rate, truly gorgeous—sat on gray concrete steps before The Sanctuary. Perfectly fitted and perfectly made up; her long auburn hair fell gently around a small and delicate face. A gown of filmy green stuff was glazed with sunlight, her breasts too small to cast a shadow. The gown crossed a stockinged calf at a casual angle. Green shoes suggested small and dancing feet. Makeup which might have been harsh in daylight was so soft her face seemed natural as a child's. A cigarette lighter shone like a dropped coin beside her. She toked on a joint. Sunlight spread like a benediction, and in the street a police car passed harmless by. The cop slumped above his steering wheel, a loafing and sleepy nemesis.

In those days I was young and in love, fascinated with sex, yet fearful; and awash in the fecundity of spring. There was something both horrible and strange about lusting after a man who had shaped himself as a woman. And, of course, it was not the man—or even the woman he portrayed—but the illusion that tightened my groin and made me laugh in a silly way. My friend and I passed silent by, turned another corner, resumed our lives. I did not even think of The Sanctuary for years, not even when grotesque murder began to walk widely along the street.

My lover's career eventually took off, and so she had to leave. She now succeeds in New York City. My own career descended to the crazy gravity, the take and retake of television commercials. I became renowned in the TV trade, selling countless Fords, hairsprays, ready-made suits, plane tickets to Bermuda or Topeka, dating services for the wistful, and public spots in behalf of wildlife, elder citizens, African orphans, condoms distributed to teenagers. Good and Evil, the Divine and the Silly, run paths through my career. Perhaps I did not do too much damage. I'd like to believe that, while knowing the truth is elsewhere. I recoil from my sleazier deeds.

In addition, a man gets tired, even when the pay is adequate. If one gets the right kind of push, one is likely to chuck the whole business.

The push arrived. For over ten years this city lay shocked by a regular series of murders. Corpses of young women appeared among dense shrubbery in remote sections of the countryside. Police could never find a freshly murdered corpse, only remains. The murderer killed, took vacations, returned to kill some more. Many of the victims were runaway girls or prostitutes, but some were not. Polite people became alarmed. TV anchors developed looks of woe to be tuned in as needed.

Then I did a radio spot for a cheap-shot horror movie. In the movie the inevitable female victims were found wearing black ribbons at their wrists. Corpses continued to appear in the surrounding countryside, but now they were ornamented with black ribbons. The murderer, or someone, returned to decorate the dead.

My father was a preacher. Some early training never completely disappears. I felt self-implicated—at least, self-associated—in murder. Guilt drove me, fatigue drove me. In moral confusion I banked my gains and tried to cut my losses. I fled to the silence of The Sanctuary.

Murders most foul. They are concluded now, the conclusion coming just before the cleansing days of Lent. The murderer is dispatched to hellish eternity, and so, perhaps, am I; but let us have one more performance. Enter with me into this theatre, the street, and let us walk through our play together. Although we speak of the recent past, let us stroll in present tense.

The world's a stage. That is not new news. We are all audience and actors, we strut and fret, the whole damned thing is theatre. I actually used to believe that.

II
THE SET

Dutch immigrants built The Sanctuary in 1901. It was not called a sanctuary then, but the Dutch Reformed Church. Their Dutch streets were squared to the last millimeter. Even today the cut and fitted stones of those original streets remain, covered with macadam. On wet nights in this Pacific Northwest, when streetlights chase shadows, and as emergency vans clang toward a hospital a mile off, I watch from the belltower as if seeing a stage on which the past plays to an emptying house.

The Dutch have a reputation for being hard-headed—or block-headed. These Vandermeers and Van Loons and Van Pelts cling to their small houses no less firmly than New York patroons once grasped their thousands of acres. In this city of immigrant Yankees, Orientals, Russians, Scandinavians, Germans, Irish, Mexicans, Eskimos and Indians, only the Yankees and the Dutch remain in place decade on decade. Yankees own grand houses on the hills. Dutch own lowland where sirens howl. Even today, every fifth or sixth house in this bleak neighborhood glistens with fresh paint. Its sidewalks are swept, its gutters flushed. Its windows gleam, and the name on the mailbox is "Van this" or "Van that." As the old neighborhood emptied, and Mexicans moved in, church congregations dwindled. Younger Dutch built a new church on higher ground, or else joined the Episcopals. The Sanctuary was desanctified; the ground floor boarded up, gray outer walls turned to flaming billboards of graffiti.

Desanctification is the way preachers and congregations ease their conscience when abandoning a church. They pretend the act wipes away all spirits. They wave a censer, say a few words, and past darkness turns to light. Say a few more words, and that which is holy changes to that which is profane. Exeunt laughing.

Even teenage hoodlums writing fuckwords on the walls with spray paint know better. The Sanctuary is as alive as Calvinist flame. All the desanctification did was allow the entry of a few demons, and, of course, those of us who seek sanctuary.

THE CAST

Five of us are regulars here. Allow me to introduce the cast. Although years come and go, and so do people, our community is fairly stable.

Our newest member is Symptomatic Nerve Gas, who takes his time a-dying from something gnawing on his liver. He is with us these past two years. Symptomatic Nerve Gas is florid and purpled and beefy. He is in his late fifties. A horror from earlier life lies athwart his brain. In Korea he saw death dealt on a scale larger than any seen by Genghis Khan. Although he sometimes speaks of other things to us, his only public words are "Symptomatic Nerve Gas" and "Felony Assault." His Army pension sustains him. He strides forth each day with field pack rolled. He wears pressed pants, denim shirts fresh from the laundry; a man of military cleanliness. He stands on street corners repeating his two phrases in a command voice. People are first shocked into avoidance. Then, familiarity brings scorn, Symptomatic Nerve Gas has an important message, but no stage presence. He breaks no laws. People mistake him for a nut.

I am in love with Silk, who would be terrified if she knew. Silk is tall, iron-haired, erect, and fleet. Her large breasts fall with the grace of poured water, for Silk is not shy. Her long legs are firmly muscled like a girl's, and she stands naked before the font some Sunday mornings. Light through stained-glass windows makes her breasts seem sacred chalices. Her hair streams to her waist, exceeding even the fall of her breasts, and what she offers—and to whom—I do not know. God or the Devil, or perhaps a patron saint. Does she offer her body, or her soul?

Silk is a private person. She was once a nun, but her church failed her through its hypocrisy. Then she was married, but the man died. Having learned hard lessons about love, she now loves small things only. The beauty of an ivory button salvaged from a discarded shirt will enthrall her for days. She collects new leaves in spring, then regards them for hours. Silk is a classy dresser who does not salvage in garbage cans or dumpsters. She rummages Yankee neighborhoods where she knows cooks, chauffeurs, yardmen, maids, and laborers. She returns with an Indian bead, or the feather from a parrot, or the discarded photograph of a kitten, now long grown to a cat, then aged to a dead cat, then to a memory.

Is it any wonder that I love her? While most of us here are beyond the compulsions of youth, yet I remain stunned on those days when sun through stained-glass windows gilds her body blue and purple and rose and gold.

By any standard of sanity or madness, Hal is probably crazy-as-hell. However, on these sacred grounds of sanctuary we do not write the standards: except, perhaps, standards of compassion. While actors take many roles, Hal settles on only one. He is seriously an English gentleman of a time before England had gentlemen; however, Hal does not understand that. Hal is celibate, thirty, dresses in medieval costumes of forest green, carries a calling horn fashioned from deer antler. His pride is a two-handed broadsword strapped over his shoulder and across his back. It is a genuine and costly Toledo blade chased by Spanish genius with dragons ornamenting steel. Its hilt shows lions rampant. He is courtly in gesture, unquestionably courageous, capable of saving maidens.

As with all of us, Hal's history is no secret. He is a remittance man. His wealthy Virginian family pays him to stay away from Virginia. We speculate that the family's wealth is such that it does not want someone around who is interested in justice.

For my own part, I admit there may be great beauty in monomania. Hal's hair is blond and long, his face thin and aristocratic. When he kneels before the altar in prayer or supplication, centuries shrug and slide away. A sense of the primeval rises, and the cross of the sword's hilt above Hal's shoulder is sensible as faith. It matches the fading cross on the altar cloth, and Hal's face is radiant.

He loves the Virgin Mary a lot more than any Dutch Calvinist ever loved her. Hal is a defender of the faith. He has never sliced a head from a body with that sword—for surely we would have heard—but he is young and strong and has prevented rapes. Should he pass you on the street do not mistake his nobility or intent.

No poet should be asked to put up with the twentieth century, but Elgin does since he's here and cannot help it. Elgin is mismatched in time. A hundred and twenty-nine years ago, when the Civil War ended, his people stood blinking in southern sunlight and faced the cold realization that they were free. They took last names—White, Black, Masters—and some of them handled freedom pretty well. Elgin would have fumbled the situation. The nineteenth century was no place for him, either. He has a shy soul, a mighty voice encased in a tiny and often muttering body. Only his words are not intimidated.

In the eighteenth century, two hundred and twenty-nine years ago, Elgin's people raised indigo around Philadelphia, tobacco in

Virginia. Yankee slave ships briskly sailed in front of Yankee winds. Slaves slaved and loved and bred and sang and died. Elgin could have done those things, but would not have excelled.

In the seventeenth century, three hundred and twenty-nine years ago, his people faced the hot green forests of the coastal south, the muddy streets of a small town named Boston. Philadelphia would not come into being for another fifteen years. Southern plantations were still unrisen from the forests. Elgin could have made a difference. He would have built original myths, stated fundamental problems. He might have been a master singer, removing puzzlement from his people. Elgin is tribal, but black folk have not been tribal for centuries.

He is a small man with a big nose and delicate hands. He dresses in denim, wears discarded blankets when he cannot find a usable coat. His big nose sniffs out the scents of poverty, of cappuccino, of salt spume blown off Puget Sound. He whiffs his celebratory way past the sour scents of winos, the Republican scents of shopping ladies, the smell of new leather from expensive stores, the warm smell of cheeses at the public market. Elgin speaks poetry on street corners. Sometimes a college jock tape-records him, then publishes the results. Elgin is said to be a great poet by those who know about such things. No one buys him a new coat, though. No one buys him a new blanket.

And then, of course, I seek sanctuary here as well, as murders accumulated along the street. You know me. I sold you your VCR, the aluminum siding for your house. You've watched me pitch discount books, records, R-rated clothing for your kids, brag about flea spray. My face once earnestly enjoined you to believe that bankers are your friends. My voice was once the voice of Jehovah, commanding your attention to the godly powers of toilet bowl cleaner. You'll also recall those days of talking beer cans, sensual waterbeds (filled, I implied, with love potions), quick and dirty diet plans. I sold steak knives, mail-order degrees in business and divinity, low-fat cheeseburgers, quickie-lubrications. During political seasons I sought your vote in behalf of mayors, senators, judges, and the death penalty.

These days I am about other matters, for actors need not be ignoble. Former colleagues shake their heads and say, "He's off his trolley." Or, they say, "This business would drive anybody nuts." Or, they say, "If I live to see retirement, I may pull the same stunt."

I master a multiplicity of roles. It is my way of seeking atonement; for I have used the sacred art of theatre to sell goods. That alone asks for atonement, but even worse, my sales in no small way helped create a killer.

Now I use the art for its own sake, keeping myself alive by nourishing art's sacred flame. Although, I confess, I am not the world's greatest actor. I am just an awfully good actor. I am an actor who walks among you with far more certainty than those first actors of recorded history, the biblical spies who Joshua sent to scout out Jericho. (You'll recall the ram's horns later blew, the walls came tumblin' down.)

I walk among you watching and waiting for the walls to crumble, although for a long time I wondered what walls you own. If you read this in a library, I may be the bleary-eyed ancient who mumbles at the next table while pretending to read the newspaper. If your business takes you to town I may be the cripple who bums you for a quarter, or a tired-looking waitress. Perhaps you read this on a bus as you travel to work. I may be the elegantly dressed woman in the seat across the aisle, or the cultured gentleman in the seat behind—the gentleman who stares forward over your shoulder.

Do not be alarmed. I'm harmless, I think. Besides, when murderers stalk your satisfied streets, what can a poor actor do to cause you fear?

ACT
ONE

III

This week I take the role of Indian wino, an aging Tlingit seduced south from Alaska by hopes of warmth and wealth. Evil things occur, and my dreams would make me weep if I did not almost understand them. I dream of killer whales, then wake to gray skies and the patter of rain pocking the surface of Puget Sound. I dream of meeting a salmon, of having the salmon hop into my arms, and he is weightless and made of clear light. The salmon and I talk together, and he explains everything. I wake with joy, then sadness, for I cannot remember his words—only know that on some level my mind understands all there is.

Another corpse has been found. A bow of black ribbon encloses the skull, like a little girl dressed for a party. This one is identified. She was Elizabeth Peterson, a diminutive Swede. On the street we called her Teeney, but she has not been on the street for almost two years. Everyone is feeling sick.

And then there is more trouble in the neighborhood. Maria Ramirez, seventeen, is missing. She is a plump and happy little girl, if still alive. We pass the Ramirez house with low mutters of apology, although we do not know why we apologize.

And Katie Van Loon may be the death of her father. She is sixteen and begins running with dopers on motorcycles. Her father is an able Dutchman. No doubt he will hammer on some dopers, and no doubt the dopers will hammer on him.

The club for homosexuals got busted this week. It sits like a neon-ornamented bed at the end of the block. The bust turned up a few drugs, plus a Yankee who works with the state ferry system. He is a man with a bureaucrat's imagination. Newspaper photographs show him bearded and wearing a housedress.

The news of Teeney's murder, plus the disappearance of Maria Ramirez, shakes the neighborhood. As the news passes along the street I sit with Elgin on the front steps of The Sanctuary. I work at carving soapstone; this piece, nearly completed, shows a seal basking on a rock. It is easy to talk to Elgin when in the role of Tlingit wino. For one thing it makes him more comfortable.

"Young ones," Elgin says, "no longer fly too near the sun. They dive right in it. Trouble be that sun is bronze, not gold." Elgin would make no black Cyrano. His big nose is wide, not long. His brow bulges as if his brain is too big for his skull. Somewhere he has obtained those big safety pins they use at stables. An old Army blanket lies pinned and snugged around him like a poncho. It places a wet and woolen smell into the misty afternoon.

Winos drink wine. The sour stink of wine mixes with the wet wool. Perhaps it does so in dispraise of Ernest and Julio, those smiling bastards who inundate this street at no inconsiderable profit to themselves. I momentarily dream of something sad and pretty. Three houses down the block last year a woman died. Eskimo woman. She gave birth, then died. Welfare workers came. They phoned Nome. A man flew down. The baby went home, back to King Island. The baby will be raised by everyone.

"Old dee-rail," I say about the wine, and take a sip. It is possible to pace this stuff. One can walk the street and fuzzily remember a pet frog one had as a boy, or think of southeast Alaska snows. There are winters up there so severe, even in southeast, one is forced to eat the dogs. Snarly dogs go first, tail-waggers last.

"Molten unmagic," Elgin whispers, and he still talks about a bronze sun, or maybe he talks about dee-rail. "Prancing, man, that's all we do. The young ones die and we be prancing. Cops say Teeney was a whore. Maybe so." Elgin does not wander in his thoughts, but he's a poet. Sometimes he speaks in shorthand. "Beware of evil women," he says, "there's something there I got to figure out." He looks at the street like a man sorrowing over the scene of a massacre. "What's back of them doors?" he asks.

Between The Sanctuary and the homosexual club lies a row of small houses. The third one belongs to Van Loon. It sparkles with blue and white paint. On either side live Ramirez and Garcia. They rent. Weeds in the yards, busted bicycles. Beyond those houses stands what we call the Soft Porn Grocery. It sells wine, Hugh Hefner, tired-looking cabbage, cigarette makings, tins of sardines or stew, week-old bread. The grocery is no bigger than the houses.

"What do you figure about demons?" Elgin asks. "Our man Hal talks witchery." Elgin's eyes are liquid as the day, and on this day the mist is nearly rain.

"Got all the demons trapped right here." I flourish the bottle. The problem with being in role is you have to stay in role. Elgin asks a good question.

"Maybe so," Elgin says, "but Hal *knows* demons, man. And Hal could ride a nightmare into ground."

On the other side of the street Vandermeer's estate stands behind chain link fence. Barbed wire runs along the top of the fence. Vandermeer owns a city lot measuring maybe 50 by 90, with a house and an enormous alder tree. His security system has blinking red eyes like the eyes of brown bears reflecting firelight. A Great Dane sometimes raises deep-throated "woofs," sometimes licks up popcorn children shove through spaces in the fence. Vandermeer trims his tiny lawn. His missus cleans up dog shit.

To the right of Vandermeer stands a new warehouse made of corrugated aluminum. It houses thousands of truck axles. I am always astounded when looking through the open loading doors. There should not be that many trucks in the whole world.

To the right of the warehouse the Cathedral Mansion Hotel rises five stories. It is old as The Sanctuary, but made of dully glowing brick. These days it houses retired men and young punks. When cops hold a bust the punks will move on. Cathedral Mansion will once more be a geriatric ghetto.

"Demons are extra old," Elgin says. "In Bible times Greeks had them, long before the coming of our Lord. The demons must of smelled fresh Hebrew meat. Otherwise, they'd of stayed Greek."

Elgin is serious. He reads a little Greek, a little Hebrew; and so do actors, but not when in the role of Indian wino.

"Demons could make you sick. They could enter your flock. Make you turn an ankle or break a leg." Elgin is not exactly explaining, he puzzles to himself. "Lift women's skirts, cause good horses to kick. Infest your bowels or cause your house to burn. They send your daughters whoring."

When Elgin gets this way I nod and sip wine. He's not often expansive. It pays to pay attention.

"Tell me we ain't got demons," he says, and motions toward the street. There are tears in his voice, if not in his eyes.

There are tears in my heart. Elgin gives his life to poetry and doesn't give crap for catching fish. He doesn't *do* anything much except see and feel and tell about it. He feels Teeney's death as badly as if she were his granddaughter. The newspapers report the murder of one more whore, and the world breathes a little easier. Elgin knows better. Teeney was important.

This week I've got an Indian's memory. This week I'm tribal. This week I figure I know who the demons are. The demons are talk. Talking's all we do. If we heard an army was coming to kill our children we'd watch it happen while we were still arguing. It's always been that way with Indians.

Behind me The Sanctuary rises into gray sky. There are voices up there, talking, talking, talking; occasional screams. Maybe the voices are only in my head. I know one thing. A lot of them don't speak Dutch.

"And now there is Maria Ramirez," Elgin says. "Could be dead. Could be a runaway."

"We'll do good," I tell him, and know he understands. All of us are looking. Hal walks everywhere, but mostly his domains are in the parks. Silk covers the Yankee neighborhoods. This week I live on the street. Symptomatic Nerve Gas spends his days downtown where there are crowds. Elgin drifts. You never know where Elgin's nose will take him. In addition, Mexicans are pretty good with their own. Folks are watching. If Maria is on the street one of us will find her. If she's dead the police will someday discover her ornamented in black ribbon.

Day fades. I have to visit Soapstone Charlie and sell this seal I'm carving before he closes his store. When in the role of Indian wino I earn my keep like any wino. I can't use the lots of money in the bank. It would mess up the role.

Soapstone Charlie runs an Indian arts and crafts store on the waterfront. He's got two tons of soapstone in his basement. If he trusts you he'll let you have a little block for carving. If he don't trust you then you have to carve in a little room in back of the store. This seal I'm carving brings me four bucks. Charlie will sell it for fifty. As he points out, he's got overhead.

Seal here in my hands is nearly complete. I feel the smoothness of his water-slick hide. Seal is a clever fellow. Sometimes he's too smart for his own good. Through the fuzz of wine I think of the fishery, of long-lining, how the baited hooks go out from the tub. They reach deep down where halibut work trails through darkness. Maybe a two-hundred-hook line. Sometimes Seal finds one of those lines. I remember seeing the lines come into the boat, and Seal has followed them nipping off fish. The lines come aboard with fish heads gaping, nothing but heads left. Seal rolls beneath

17

the water. Laughs with a full belly. Then fishermen shoot him with a 30-30.

Seal is a happy fellow mostly. Here, all water-smooth in my hands, I feel him laugh. Four bucks buys supper and two bottles.

IV

The street with rain is easier, and the route to Soapstone Charlie's is direct. In the next block there's a bus shelter where younger winos meet. Half of them are black dudes, also some Mex and Puerto Rican. Tough, tough assholes, except wine has a way of making everybody not so tough. These guys are sonsovbitches, though. Pass out and they'll steal your shoes. Sometimes they'll steal them anyway. Indians avoid them.

When gray mist turns to rain people huddle in doorways of abandoned buildings. Waste paper on the street turns wet and gray. Slop floats in gutters, while the downtown empties of people asking for handouts. Tired beggar women pack up tired children and magically disappear. Barefoot punks put away signs reading "I'm not drunk, just hungry." If a little wind rises behind the rain the street is safe. Dopers are owlshit. Afraid to get their feet wet.

Elgin says we have demons. Elgin says Hal is talking about demons.

What Elgin knows—probably—and what Hal never will know—probably—is that "demon" is a catchall word. In the old,

old days when demons had some credit, they could be spirits of the dead, or they could be spirits that had never technically been alive. They could take the forms of cats, necromancers, beautiful women; and they could be savage things that took shapes with fangs and shrieks. They could be incubus or succubus. They could take the forms of tiny babies. The old dark days of superstition were filled with demons. Today we mostly have political terrorists. Same principle. Stark, unexplained, unreasoning horror.

And Elgin says we have demons. Hal talks about demons. For all the dark centuries Hal knows about, there have been witches and warlocks. For all the dark centuries that Indians know about, there have been the same. The difference is that Indians have something more. Our shamans have more power than priests. Indians have a sense of balance. The Eskimo woman who died giving birth might have become a demon. Still, everybody knew she wouldn't, even if she had a right. We all felt sorry for her. Her baby was taken in.

Thinking this way is like being in a wino dream, walking toward Soapstone Charlie's. I remember a town named Klawock on Prince of Wales Island. There was a totem park up there standing on a hill, nineteen totems including Raven and Whale sailing in a gray and rainy sky. Down below, on the side of the hill, was an abandoned Presbyterian church. Its steeple rose to the sky. The totems were all rotted out at the top, the cross on the church broken and skewed.

It's the same sort of thing at The Sanctuary. When gray light falls through broken stained-glass windows, the high-arching ceiling is covered with darkness and shadow. There are voices up there which violate the church. Something got into The Sanctuary either before the desanctification or afterward. I know they were there before Hal showed up.

Hal just walked in one day about three years ago, knelt before the altar and crossed himself. Hal did not wear forest green at the time. His brown jerkin was darker than sackcloth. His shirt was fringed along the sleeves so movement handling the sword would not be impeded. Hal's blond, nearly white hair glowed before the altar, and the hair flowed to his waist. No one else was around, except Silk, who sat in a pew before the font examining three marbles. One was striped red, one blue, and one a "cleary." I slept in the sacristy, which is where I live; and Hal's low prayer brought me awake. No one sleeps deep in sanctuaries.

"And by the sacred cross, I swear," Hal said, "before this portal of God . . . ," but, at the time, we did not know what he swore to, nor did we know his spirit's depth. This stranger stood among us, and we saw, without the aid of help or benison, that madness lived.

"Holy Mother, with thy aid along my arm . . ."—and Hal flourished his strong hands—". . . will defend thy children."

"If you take that weapon into the street," Silk told him gently, "the police will put you four floors *under* the jail."

What is memorable was their faces. Perhaps that is really the day when I fell in love with Silk.

She has never been a mother, although as a nun she was the wife of Christ. Then, latterly, she was wife to a man who ran an auto electric shop all his life. The bishops of the church got between her and her Lord. Death got between her and her man. Maybe if she'd had a child she would be different. Hal's madness was so pure it stirred Silk from her preoccupations.

There's a look some women get that lives beyond tenderness, and Silk's face carried the serenity of that look. You see it in old paintings, sometimes. It is the look of a thirteenth-century Madonna, and it carries the wisdom of love and hearth, creative energy, the sensibleness of grain fields. It is the face of ancient goddesses, but modern women will not even know what I mean. A few actresses perhaps, or maybe a few poets. Men understand it, though, cherish the singular memory of such a look through decades of their lives.

Silk's face is remarkable because it is such a contrast to her body. The face is delicate, the body over-breasted with nipples large and long. Pubic hair lies rampant between those firm legs.

21

Her crotch is wide, her belly tight, her armpits full and alive with hair. She is the very essence of fecundity, and above such a body a delicate face floats like a Shakespearean moon rising thinly above ramparts.

Her voice was gentle as her face. "You are a defender, then?" she asked Hal. "Not an avenger. I've never understood avengers." Silk's mouth is narrow but generous. Her lips seem made for whispering.

Hal was startled. In his monomania he was surely accustomed to jeers, to stares, to the ignorance of those who read the newspapers each morning to find out who they will be that day. Now—and here—a woman reached toward his understanding, someone who saw him as wonderful; someone who could see that a defender was important and an avenger was not. It is an old, old distinction. Centuries seemed to rise between Silk and Hal. Hal fell to his knees before her. "My Lady."

His face is also narrow, his lips soft and untested as a young boy. His frame is large, but supple as innocence, and he moves with innocence. Hal's hands are strong, his arms fully muscled, but the face is like a face cloistered in stained glass. It carries no fatuous ignorance like a choirboy. Instead, it holds young idealism that has met its first hard tests and survived. Hal's eyes are nearly chocolate, but their darkness holds light and energy. The dark eyes and the white-blond hair are focal, illuminating shadows of The Sanctuary.

Silk gently laid her hand upon Hal's head. It was a mother's touch, not imperious or royal. From beyond The Sanctuary came the rising shouts of two amigos speaking Spanish. Rows of pews stood ranked like petitioners, and from the street a siren opened, then choked. Red and blue lights flashed in the gray mist. Children paused in their play. From a distance Vandermeer's Great Dane woofed.

"Let us sit before the altar," Silk said to Hal. "And you will say from what land you hail, and who you are. It will make me happy."

* * *

That was three years ago. For three years Hal has walked the streets, and even dopers do not frig with him. Nor do the police. Maybe cops think the sword is a toy. Maybe they think Hal doesn't know how to use it. They certainly write him off as helpless. Maybe the cops are just relieved to see a simple sword carried openly. The dopers carry automatic pistols.

Hal has prevented rapes. He brings lost children to their parents. Old people in the neighborhood can go shopping without being mugged. In preventing rapes Hal has doubtless prevented murders or body-rending assaults. He sure didn't save Teeney, though. Teeney is dead.

V

Her face is everywhere along this street. People pass and don't see her, but those people never paid attention when she was alive. They come and go, our young ones like Teeney; and, as Elgin says, we pay no attention because we are too busy prancing. Truth to tell, though, every Teeney out here is our daughter. We're not taking care of our daughters. Teeney's slim form is wraithlike as it moves along the nearly deserted street. She was such a little bitty girl. It's just natural her spirit would be little. Maybe Teeney has become a demon.

Maybe all those murdered girls have become demons. There are more than forty murdered girls so far, and maybe they all whisk along this street looking for their murderer. If that's true they don't have far to look. The murderer could be anybody, but you can bet he's out here. If he is not in the street right now, if he's in jail or something, you can bet his cousin is right around the corner.

Walking toward Soapstone Charlie's I ask myself what in the *world* am I doing here? This place is too big and ugly for an Indian.

Then a split in my mind takes over. The actor part of me starts watching the part of me that's in the role of Indian. The actor part does not intrude into the role, but it *watches* the role. It sees the Indian part, just like the actor is also part of the audience. My mind widens and becomes all-seeing, like I was a Tlingit grave guardian protecting against witches. When I start telling about it I can tell more, because I *see* more. It goes like this:

A weather system, more gray and ancient than a solitary old Indian, rolls from the Pacific across mountain ranges that have stood ten million years. The weather breeds in the Aleutian Islands, moving south and east as it bumps against the coasts of Alaska and Canada, the weather roiled and turbulent with rain. Wind raises whitecaps across the wide and Indian face of Puget Sound, and rain speckles whitecaps with small pluckings in the susurrant rush of water. Rain blows against the faces of tall buildings in the city, and it runs down the trunks of ancient trees. As darkness closes its jaws on the city, electric lights become brilliant in primary colors. In the parks, burrows of small animals flood. Mice and shrews are forced to take wet cover above ground, and they stand huddled and blinking in the rain.

The city, itself, is long and narrow. It carries a freeway the length of its spine, and is enclosed by lakes. At this time of day helicopters rise from a nearby airport. They chip-chip-chip through low skies, monitoring the freeways. Radio announcers jive with the pilots, and the pilots tell soon-to-be-homeward-bound workers which roads are open. Taillights are like the eyes of demons as they flash in tens of thousands through the mist.

And demons congregate. In this great city spires of churches spell out the earth's religions. There are crosses upon crosses upon crosses. Some of the crosses are double-barred above the onion domes of Russian churches. There are simple crosses everywhere; and, here and there in churches or museums, are the Cross Patee, the Cross Byzantine, even the Maltese Cross. There are replicas of ancient crosses put into modern architecture by architects either devout or show-off, the Tau Cross, also the cross of the eternally damn'ed Irish charged with a shamrock leaf—while in the shrines of bus kiosks festers the most primitive cross of all, startling in black spray paint: the Flyflot pre-Christian Cross, these days known as a Swastika.

There are cathedrals here, and mosques. There are Buddhists, Muslims; while Indian totems rise in the parks. There are Shinto shrines and shrines to the Holy Mother. There are black gods and white gods and oriental gods; and demons stream in the sky above the churches. The helicopter pilots do not see them, the commuters are too busy following taillights.

An old Indian pauses momentarily before the bus station. He peers into the waiting room where street punks and bag ladies wait out the weather. Tired mothers perch tired children on suitcases so neither will be stolen. Television screens glow, as waiting commuters drop two-bits in slots, then sit on hard plastic seats of purchased privacy like cockpits with TV as the control panel. They catch the top of the evening news. The old Indian sees a 1/100th of a second hesitation in a commercial depicting a spontaneous action. He mutters to the rain that the entire industry is getting sloppy when such work gets by. Then he grunts, touches the smoothness of a carved seal in the depth of his jacket pocket. The commercial ends. A still photo is shown. A girl is missing. The news anchor attempts to sound distressed.

The missing girl is a Yankee. Of course, she cannot help that. An accident of birth.

Maria Ramirez' face is not on television. No search is planned for her. On the other hand, no television news anchor is expressing bullshit concern. It seems to the old Indian that everything is this city is either plus or minus. As he walks through the rain-ridden early evening he keeps a bleared eye open for Maria.

And all across the city *stuff* happens.

Katie Van Loon, the sixteen-year-old who has started running with bikers, has had her first screw and can't figure what to think, because it was supposed to be fun. She sits on the rug in the middle of a small room at Cathedral Mansion Hotel. Her blond hair is bobbed, her shoulders and thighs heavy, her face blank, her breasts unflattering, her toes curled. She is only slightly stoned, but the guy lights up. If she's lucky the guy will beat on her, but only a little. Then she will learn. If she learns she will probably go home and shut her face about what she knows. Her father will not tangle with the bikers. Someday she will meet a nice Dutchman. It all depends on whether she learns the old commercial adage, "You can pay me now or you can pay me later."

In the middle of downtown, Symptomatic Nerve Gas has already put in nine hours on the street. Now begins the busiest part of his day. Commuters' heels click along concrete paths to their cars. Parking garages empty. The commuters are overloaded with office talk and machinations and petty politics. Half of them fear for their jobs, and the other half would be relieved if they were fired . . . or, perhaps that is a fool assumption. They must *like* what they do, or they wouldn't do it year after year. Symptomatic Nerve Gas has a hard time commanding their attention. He stands militant on a street corner, pushing his two phrases through the gray rain in a command voice. For him, the rain is nothing.

He will never forget the retreat from P'yŏngyang. How Chinese, not Koreans, came in solid streams along roads and were gunned down, the metallic glaze of uniforms frosting as they fell, dead faces freezing to unoriental white. His was a small and important action along the ice of the Taedong River, although he did not know it was important at the time. All he knew was that if his feet froze he was a dead man. Fifty Chinese divisions massed just above the Thirty-eighth Parallel. Five UN divisions opposed them in a defense perimeter around Seoul. He would not have gotten out, except for a lucky ride with a group of retreating Brits. Later, they were joined by a battalion of Greeks. Symptomatic Nerve Gas looks at commuter faces which have never seen war. His imagination shows those faces lying in the streets, washed by rain. The average body contains six quarts of blood, six thousand quarts per thousand people. Symptomatic Nerve Gas knows how a thousand drained bodies look. He sees gutters washing with blood, sidewalks stained, the rain no greater than a whisk broom sweeping at torrents of blood. He is an inarticulate man with a great message, and so he does his best.

And all across the city *stuff* happens.

Theresa Ramirez is Maria Ramirez' mother. She mourns and fears and praises with her hands. They are presently busy rolling and slapping tough dough enclosing beans for the evening meal. Three young children, Maria's two brothers and little sister, sit before television in the living room of the small house. The tower of The Sanctuary rises nearby. Theresa's heavy face is mixed with Indian blood, her heavy lips firm against tears and terror as she slaps dough and stares into the wet back yard. Maria is out there somewhere, but Theresa cannot abandon these children. She cannot walk streets looking for her daughter.

Her husband will return from work. He will eat, shrug, make a disgruntled remark about Jesus. Then he will walk dark streets and search until midnight. Jorge Ramirez will be a small and dark-haired man checking the bars and topless, a dark-skinned little man. Teeney's father was not large, either. He was a blond and worried little man who checked bars for a year. At midnight Jorge will return to sleep. At six A.M. he will head for the day labor pool.

Television shows the picture of a missing Yankee girl. Theresa wonders if television would show Maria's picture; but her's is vague wondering. Television is not for Mexicans. Theresa does not know why she knows that. Perhaps her Indian blood is wise.

28 Hal has spent the day looking for Maria while attending to his other duties. Rain glistens on Hal's forest green cap. His nearly white hair ties at the base of his skull and again at the ends. He does not braid his hair, and the hair is darker with the rain. Hal stands alert in a plaza before a bank. Modern sculpture raises aluminum

wings before darkened windows. Along the walls of the bank tall rhododendrons and taller sycamores offer parklike cover for sleeping men, or men concealed to attack any woman careless enough to cross the plaza. Hal does not think of rapists. He thinks of trolls, and perhaps there is not that much difference. In this fresh darkness Hal watches well-manicured women assemble at a bus stop half a block away. Hal will stand as their defender until rush hour is over. This is his post at this time of day. The plaza is famous for rapes.

When rush hour ceases Hal will walk briskly—he always walks briskly—to The Sanctuary. He will perform his religious duties, then eat cheese and beef and bread, washed by two bottles of beer. He sleeps wrapped in a blanket on a hard pew. The Sanctuary has no heat. Night is abated by candles. At five A.M. Hal will rise, perform his religious duties, cleanse himself, and step into the dark morning for the first of his rounds. He goes to a nearby grade school where, last year, two children were molested in an ugly manner. Hal stands across the street and watches until all children are safely inside.

But Hal will not do that until morning. Right now night grows heavier. The slap-slap-slap of a siren in the distance screams 'emergency.' Somewhere, somebody is down. Heart attack, maybe, or stabbed; maybe an overdose. The siren whacks at the rain and dark.

Along the street commuter cars slow, stop, while money and drugs change hands. These are the pisspot twenty-to-fifty-buck sales, hash and marijuana. These are also the commuters without many connections, or those who hate their lives so much they'd deal with a Jamaican. On the flip side, though, these commuters are old hands with drugs. They can tell right away if something's laced. This is the Toyota and Volkswagen crowd. The big shots buy at the office.

Belov'ed Silk walks easy through the rain. She returns to The Sanctuary like a busy wife home to cook dinner for her family. Silk wears a swell raincoat discarded by some woman who had too many, and she carries an umbrella. Beneath streetlights her polished shoes are twinkly. Silk's moves are street-smart. They intimidate punks. Since no street punk is certain of much, Silk's confidence alarms them.

Silk scored twice today. The first score nestles in her coat pocket. It is a 1926 Studebaker hubcap no larger than a small ashtray. She feels steel threads as she cherishes the metal with her fingers. This is a hubcap you couldn't lose, because it screwed onto the hub. She runs her fingers across the face of the hubcap, enameled indentations spelling out the name. A chauffeur in the Yankee neighborhoods found it in the attic of a garage. He polished and saved it, knowing Silk would be pleased.

Silk's second score is the knowledge that Maria Ramirez was still alive as late as yesterday. Probably. The security man at a wealthy retirement home saw a stubby Mexican girl riding in a black van. He noticed her after the van passed the retirement home a third time. His training said someone looked for something to steal. He tried to make out the driver but could not. He is certain about the girl.

It is bad and good news. If Maria, then surely she is a runaway. The Ramirez family will take that hard. At the same time, it is good news because Maria is not stolen and killed. Probably.

Silk must decide whether Ramirez should know. Silk understands the pain of hope. She knows hope keeps a person nailed in place. It keeps one in convent long after eternal spirits have fled. It makes one try to breathe life into an obviously dying man.

This treasure in her pocket, this small hubcap, will neither die nor change. It may get lost or stolen, but in Silk's imagination it will remain what it is forever. It is already far older than Silk.

Religion changes, though, although maybe God does not. Silk still tries to figure that one out. Men change. Even the street changes. Almost everything changes. No one builds Studebakers any more.

Yet, Silk does not despair. As she heads for The Sanctuary, she goes in the knowledge that in Yankee neighborhoods the word is out. Servants and service people watch for Maria. Silk puzzles the situation. She expects the Yankees to alienate their own children, for they alienate everyone else. She does not expect that sort of thing among Mexicans.

Murder may be the greatest moral crime, but it may not be the most obscene. Which is more obscene? Someone who kills, or someone who decorates corpses? In an abstract way the question is apt. The whole business of television is really the business of ornamenting corpses. Take commercials as a starting place: in ads for vitamins, Eve tells Adam she's awfully careful about what she takes into her body. When the topic is junk food, Vincent van Gogh would give more than just his ear to feast on a particular cheeseburger (Van goes for it); and when Moses parts the Red Sea it is in search of a certain brand of pickled herring.

The Russians, it is said, rewrite history. How different they are from Americans. In America history is murdered. Our gods and heroes are used to sell soap.

Do such thoughts occur to an old Indian as he leaves a waterfront store? Four one-dollar bills nest like crumpled feathers in the lining of his coat. He mutters, retraces his steps, heads for the cheapo wine shelf at the Soft Porn Grocery.

Thus day ends and night begins. Commuters' taillights brighten like demonic eyes. Rain (that cannot wash sorrows) washes the street. It penetrates the wool blanket snugged around Elgin's shoulders while he sniffs scents of rain, fish, oil, hemp, and gull droppings along a deserted pier. Smells congregate and his nose separates them, finding proper origins for each. Elgin looks into the dark void of Puget Sound, his eyes moist with tears not rain. He will search for Maria in the morning, but this day is no doubt the last set aside, by anyone, exclusively for Teeney. Teeney was a daughter of our tribe. Elgin murmurs, but no college jock is there to hear.

31

Where has the white bird flown,
who was our child?
Are white wings folded, and her song,
and ours,
stilled before ruckus and neon?
Or,
do we tune instruments, clear throats
for her accompaniment,
of our shriek wild above wet gutters
and beneath steeples?
Lamentation of busted skulls,
poorly bones, marrow dry,
heads varicose with prance and jive,
our deaths, not hers, our dirge.

VI

Tit and clit and cock and ball. At night the street heats up. Bulbs on marquees light with messages: "Topless and Bottomless" or "The Dirtiest Show in Town"—but the real messages are: there is no let or end to perversity. There are a thousand ways to twist and sell. The street knows all those ways.

Showtime. *Up-time. Down-time. High-time.* The evening's fun features bevies of beauties, death-defying acts in Cadillacs, lines of coke snorted in naked-fanny glory at rent-by-hour motels.

Tonight the street scratches its usual January rash. The weather is late winter, early spring; frost in the mornings, with robins winging singly in as here and there sprouts crocus. Next month brings Fat Tuesday, this town's Mardi Gras. There will be costumes and a parade; then everybody will get flat-ass drunk. Tonight we just have the usual stuff.

Sally's Army entertains; a Mighty Fortress–type of hymn presses into the rain from one trombone, one clarinet, one tambourine, and a pair of knocking sticks. The Army stands across the street, black and red uniforms, music thumping past canned music of stereos from passing cars, past bleats of pullers-in before the clubs—those sharkskin dudes with sharkskin eyes who yell "Home of the E Cup," or, "Brother, this is Titty City."

I sit in the entry of a closed pawnshop beside two other winos, and remember Teeney. Teeney was not a whore. She hung around the bars. She looked for love, and maybe she had love and sex all mixed up. Being young is very hard.

I've sat with these two guys before. The entry to the pawnshop is shelter against foggy rain, and in the street headlights spread bright layers of glisten beneath colored signs of bars. The two guys with me are pretty well dee-railed. One has a bottle, the other has a half. I've got one, plus another stashed, but don't mind sharing. I'm Tlingit. This is a potlatch.

The gentleman to my right is a Haida. Haidas and Tlingits generally don't mix. Haidas are too mean, but Jimmy's an exception. He's a skinny little guy in his thirties, and I guess there's Flip mixed in with the Indian. There's an awful lot of Filipinos in Alaska. Jimmy's turning into a ghost right before our eyes. That's not a white man's metaphor. It's an Indian fact. We have a yek, a sacred animal with us.

Land Otter is a big yek among the Tlingit. For the last half hour Jimmy's been hallucinating Land Otter; but now, what's even worse, it's stopped being hallucination. At least I think so. Jimmy seems to know that Land Otter really is here. Plus, Haidas will steal anything.

A yek is a power animal. Call it a totem. Land Otter is powerful because he goes beyond nature. Among Indians there are animals of water or land or air. Land Otter doesn't fit. He's elemental on land *and* in water. I feel nearly stilled in the presence of Land Otter. I'm afraid I'll start to see him. He has plenty of power.

The patriarchal gent to my left is Tex, who most likely hails from Arkansas. His main claim is a miracle liver. Either that or he's got more than one liver. Tex is past seventy. He got shot down in World War II. Twice. He was aft gunner in a B-17. In the first crash seven guys died and Tex got a broken ankle. In the second crash they made it back to base, then burned. Three guys got out, but Tex was fried real, real bad. It makes me hurt and fear just to think about it. Tex's face looks normal and old-man-raggedy on one side, looks like smooth and dirty paper on the other. Part of his head has hair. He still has one ear.

"His tongue's sticking out." Jimmy isn't screaming or flopping around. He looks like a tired pile of rags, or maybe a dying rabbit. His face is too flat, even for an Indian. If he's terrified he manages to keep it to himself. If this is not hallucination, if Land Otter really is here, Land Otter may be playing games with Jimmy; but if Land Otter's tongue is out it probably isn't a game. Tlingits know the tongue is where life enters, but it's also where life leaves. I think Jimmy is going to die pretty soon. Maybe tonight. Land Otter tells him something. It isn't likely Land Otter brings good news.

Across the street sits a wino wearing two topcoats and a red felt hat. People call him "Post Office" or "Drop." He makes his living as a message center. He's got a fantastic memory. Dopers give him a few bucks to pass information. He's strictly rotten fish.

Two girls stand at the curb while headlights flame along wet pavement. One is fourteen or fifteen, a thickset Indian, probably born down here. No one raised in Alaskan villages could catch on this fast. Indian faces generally aren't hard, but this child is not soapstone, she's granite. She carries that unkillable look the young kids get, and she probably thinks it means something. It doesn't. Anybody can kill a whore. The police don't care. These days it's a buyer's market for pimps.

The second girl is about sixteen and dishwater blonde, tall with legs so good she could do commercials. It's a pleasure to see such legs and not have to do anything except appreciate. More and more girls travel and sell in pairs, and this pair is a smorgasbord of the streets. The Indian girl has big tits, the white girl little ones; but those miraculous legs. Things like that count out here.

"I fucked every color of girl there is in the world, plus a hundred head of cattle more or less. If I could of taught a goat in Montana to cook I'd of never got married." Tex points to the dishwater blonde. "I must of fucked fifty like that before I caught on. Back when I was a young rooster."

"I wish I was hunting mushrooms," Jimmy says, and sounds like he's explaining something to Land Otter. "Or fishing."

"They wasn't nothin' but girl whores back them days," Tex says. "None of these skinny little queer-punks."

"I don't like this shit," I say. The problem with being in role is you have to stay in role. Sometimes the role takes you places you don't want to visit. I don't want to think of Land Otter. I don't see any reason why Jimmy ought to die.

"These days you can't tell the difference," Tex says. "I heard about this guy got changed to a woman and didn't care for it. So he got changed so he wasn't either. Queer stuff. It was in a newspaper."

I could call 911. It's a free call. But, if I call 911 that breaks the role. And, even if I do call 911, they aren't going to help Jimmy. Nine-eleven will just throw him into detox. We need a shaman, and there are no shamans at detox.

This chemical wine makes my head feel like it's got tight-stretched wires pulling back and forth. It's not a normal drunken feeling. The best bet for Jimmy is to puke and pass out. Maybe Land Otter will be disgusted. Then he'll leave.

"What'd you catch on to?" I ask Tex, because he may have been a smart man once. Even now, an old, old wino, he has flashes.

"Whores want to die. Fucking is a way of getting killed."

Tex's words make me sick and drunker. The whole street is a death trip. I see it now. Only Salvation Army sounds the news of resurrection with brass and cymbal—and it don't sound convincing.

Only the passage of time is going to get rid of this wine. Only time is going to take the snap and tension from these wires. I don't have to spend that time here. Somewhere else may not hurt any less than here, but maybe it will be different.

It hurts to stand. At least the knees and ankles tell me they hurt, even when the wine says they don't. Mixed signals along the wires. I pretend to be drunker than I am, to the point it's possible to leave the bottle sitting beside Jimmy. "I'll be back," I tell them, and they know it's true or the bottle would not sit there. As it is, they'll lick it dry. I'm dangerously close to coming out of role, just drunk enough not to care.

They sit, Jimmy and Tex, and probably Land Otter too. The darkened windows of the hockshop strut festoons of junk. An old sextant lies beside an accordion. A trumpet hangs from a wire, like a tool of Gabriel about to blow Jimmy home. Jimmy don't know anything about Gabriel, except what Salvation Army tells him.

It hurts to walk, but not too much. "Go home," I mutter to the two girls as I pass them, my mutter so low they cannot hear. If they hear they'll call names and spit. The rain is really mist, but there's enough of it these kids will get driven to shelter pretty quick if they're not picked up. They're too young to get into bars, even on this street, not too young to do business in the back rooms of bars.

I stand on the corner watching traffic. We've got a real show tonight. It's Looney Tunes and Merrie Melodies. The band across the street blows strong. A Sally-lady passes pamphlets, while in the next block a Southern street preacher yells damnation, not redemption. He's got his congregation with him. All he lacks is a tent. This preacher has his own wrinkle, his gimmick. His followers pass out balloons—red, yellow, green—reading "Repent" and "Glory" and "Praise Him." Some of the street punks get with his program. They carry balloons, or pop them with lighted cigarettes. It's like a carnival with all those balloons dancing in the rain.

Traffic cruises past. Some of the drivers just cruise, vaguely wondering about action. Some of them are johns, checking out the women. The johns are just as screwed up as the girls. Give me a television set and I can sell them anything.

They're losers, these johns. Or maybe some are seekers after truth. Guys in their thirties to fifties suffering prolonged adolescence and the loneliness that goes with it. Powerlessness drives them. They cruise with peckers perpetually at half mast, the truest examples of The American Dream.

Man, they are Consumers. What they can't screw they'll wear, and what they can't wear they'll drink, and what they can't drink they'll attend at the price of the ticket. Indians have forgotten more about power than these johns will ever know.

And, of course, a few of them are murderers. I'm reminded of this because something awful happens. It doesn't sober me. Only time will do that—but it churns me, the adrenalin gets in a big fight with the wine. My eyes sharpen. I really *see* this street.

A black van cruises past. It's one of those big humpers, all shiny and chrome. One of those studly bedrooms on wheels. It carries a custom paint job. A satanic face is surrounded by flames; and there must be a dozen vans like this, with faces like this, on the street right now. Painted flames surround the painted face. The van has those black windows so the driver can see out but people can't see in. Junk like this infests the street. This van, though, has the rider's window rolled down.

Teeney sits in that van, alive as can be. I see her. I don't believe it, but I see her so well I've got to believe it. Teeney's not dead after all. Teeney is even laughing, and she turns toward the driver like she talks about something silly. The van moves slow because of traffic, but faster than a man can run.

I stumble after it, back the way I came, chasing the van, cursing my drunken legs; past the two whores, past Jimmy and Tex and Land Otter and the pawnshop. I run for a whole block as white lights blaze off pavement, with the thump of Sally-music crashing against my skull, with a sudden heavy wave of hashish smelling from somewhere. My breath gives out. I fall against a mailbox and grab hold. The mailbox is wet and slick, but I'm kind of draped over it. The van winks its taillights, hangs a left two blocks down the street.

Why in hell am I crying? Tears all across my face like rain. Not tears you'd want to wipe away. You don't wipe away thanks. Or miracles. Teeney's alive.

The guy may be cruising. I tell myself, Hang onto this mailbox and wait. What goes around comes around. Maybe this gent is going around.

Of course he's going around. The first law of the street is to keep moving. There are good reasons for that law. Maybe I'll think about them sometime. Right now I think of our children, and especially of Teeney.

Most young girls are pretty, but so ignorant their eyes carry flat looks. Their brains have not yet been used for much. Mouths hold perpetual pouts. Voices reveal low-level hysteria when they try to speak softly, so mostly they talk too loud or yell. These, our daughters—and even the Yankee girls are our daughters—resemble breeding stock.

Teeney is different. Even at her age, which must be twenty by now, light rises deep from her eyes. Her face is little because she is little. Her forehead is high and also narrow. She has a small mole on the back of her right hand. Blue eyes, flat Scandinavian bone structure about her cheeks, a strong chin. When she laughs or makes jokes, her eyes light with confidence, because half of what makes her happy is knowing she's making you happy. There is just more *to* Teeney than to most young girls.

I stand holding the mailbox like it was a chubby dance partner. Pretty soon the flat nose of that van will rise behind these cars that all seem stamped by Japanese cookie cutters. This time around I'll yell and wave. Teeney will tell the guy to pull over. We will say "Hello" and "You're alive" and "Of course I'm alive, just up from Mendocino" and "Silk will be so glad. She's prayed" and "I'll come by and see her tomorrow." Yes, it will be that way. Of course it will.

Of course it will.

Meanwhile, shit happens.

You cannot get away from them these days. They infest, less easily dealt with than locust; and, like locust they run on clack and whirr. Among TV snoops there's something missing, some crooked illness of mind. The best that can be said is some are less ill than others, but none avoid brain death. I recognize the portable lights without even turning my head. My ears pick up the chatter. A field crew raids this neighborhood. They no doubt do an "in-depth" report on the street. You can do nothing in-depth for an hour of TV.

It takes more than an hour to really experience one of Elgin's poems.

I let go of the mailbox but do not turn. For one thing, I recognize the voices. That particular reporter is an unctuous flack. I remember her first report on the Jonestown Massacre. She ended with a silly smile and the comment, "Isn't it just bizarre the things some people do?"

My role is perfect. They will not recognize me, but—by all that was once precious—this is *my* role. I don't want them to point their camera. I don't want to be taped in the middle of a great performance. I just want to watch for Teeney.

"Is that man ill?" She's asking Tex about Jimmy. She hopes Jimmy will die on camera. To the cameraman she says, "This looks serious."

"Lady," Tex says, "I musta fucked fifty like you before I finally caught on."

Tex is a miracle. He's over seventy. He's wine-burned. He can't keep that up, but he's already said it all. The flack is good. She doesn't gasp. "That won't even edit," she says to the cameraman. "Let's move." They head for the street preacher. Balloons are everywhere.

The van is coming around. It's still a block away, but doing maybe ten miles an hour. The front of the van is painted like the sides, the painting demonic. Somebody paid a lot of money for decoration. This is not a cliché demon. This is a small, hot demon that is mostly eyes. I step to the curb. Everything's going to be all right.

The rider's window is rolled down. There's a girl sitting in the van, but she does not look like Teeney. Now the street preacher makes out before the cameras, a love fest with Jesus. The Salvation Army band rocks like the old ship of Zion. Dopers carry balloons. Someone mutters low and slow in Spanish, the vowels soft and friendly.

Maria Ramirez sits in the van. She laughs, waves to me, does not speak. My joy changes to guttural scream. We're looking for you Maria, but that is not what I scream. I just scream. The van passes. Totally indifferent. I watch it for two blocks, and it hangs a left. The guy is going around again.

Lean against the mailbox. Gasp, pull in air. Lungs cramped like hurt muscles. The wires seem so tight they'll pull the veins right out of my temples.

Maybe Teeney got out of the van, maybe Maria got in. That's wrong. It's all I've got. If I can't believe that, then anything else is too horrible. What goes around comes around. I head back in the direction the van will come from.

Tex is standing as I pass. He holds a bottle, hitting it serious. Jimmy lies there. It doesn't pay to look. A doper has tied a red balloon to Jimmy's foot, like the toe tag in a morgue. The balloon dances in the mist and movement of air. It reads "Rejoice." No sign of Land Otter. Ten steps past them Tex's voice comes chasing me. He curses everything, but now the curses are filled with terror; plus Tex is running out of breath. That TV flack should have waited.

The black van comes again. This time the window is rolled, and this time my mind is wrapped in horror.

Black ribbons fly from the radio antenna. It should be a surprise, it's only a shock. I stare hard through wine and into the deep black of the window. Nothing moves in there. Imagination shows me the picture of a skull. The skull isn't laughing. The demon painted on the side of the van *is* laughing. Black ribbons flutter in the rain.

Sanctuary. It is either get to Sanctuary or die. I don't know what I've seen and don't know what I hope. All I know is horror; and one thing more. Hell can't show anything worse than dying on the street. There's nothing I can do for Jimmy. There's nothing I can do for Teeney, for Maria, or even for myself. Only flee to Sanctuary.

ACT
TWO

VII

Days pass as mist and winter rain surround us. This Pacific Northwest is not always gray and wet, but no chamber of commerce will admit the real number of gray days. Chambers of commerce praise blue skies and mild weather. They forget unending rain, crime rates, tourist taxes, and political gee-whiz.

Sometimes we have sunshine. If sunshine goes on too long the suicide rate goes up. When everyone else seems having fun loneliness increases among lonely people. More sunglasses per capita are sold here than any other place. By the time one needs them, the last pair that got bought is lost. Plan your vacation here in August, or visit Yellowstone instead.

I've spent the week preparing a new role. I will be a fifty-eight-year-old Yankee dowager whose daughters are raised, and whose husband has a problem with cholesterol. I'll have my worries, hopes, successes. It will be time to go into role directly.

Meanwhile, there is good news and bad news. The missing Yankee girl is found. She shacked up with her uncle in Miami Beach. Her family is influential. A news cap sits atop the whole affair. The bad news is that Maria Ramirez is still missing. Silk remains hopeful.

I've said nothing about the black van, about the ghost of Teeney—if it was a ghost and not a wino vision. I've once more accepted that Teeney is dead. I've suffered the original grief twice. Sadness floods the small chamber where I live, the sacristy.

The sacristy is twelve by twelve feet. It has a large closet for ministerial robes, a locking chest for wafers of the Host, and for sacramental wine that in this century has been grape juice. Calvinist rear ends are pretty tight, their brains routine. Imagination belongs to Baptists who perform the miracle of changing wine to water.

The sacristy holds my monkish bed where Silk will never visit. It is one of those Victorian three-quarter beds made for hulking youth—a vague acknowledgment that when sperm gathers, the young need a bit more room. In its way the thought is filthy, but Victorian ornamentation averages everything out. This bed has carved roses, the headboard seven feet high, the footboard a good five feet. There's a twelve-foot ceiling here. Lots of space available if a man could fly.

On the other hand, a room this size does not get so cold as the huge and empty church. In winter, sometimes, breath is frosty and Hal wraps himself in a buffalo robe left over from one of my roles. Hal could seek smaller, thus warmer space in the church kitchen, or in one of the small meeting rooms in the basement. Or, I could buy heat and light with the lots of money in the bank, the way I now pay water bills. Hal, however, is esthetic. He sets standards. Artificial heat and light would be difficult for Hal to handle.

I would not want you to think all here is only gloomy or esthetic. Actors will tell you that, without comedy, tragedy makes little sense. Mexican children play on the steps; and, on dry evenings, all of us sometimes sit on the steps watching the parade of lovelies head for the homosexual bar. I have taught Hal some appropriate expressions: "Hey Nonney Nonney."

Symptomatic Nerve Gas has traveled, and on some evenings

tells stories from across the world. Silk knows jokes about bishops. I once wanted to be trumpeter in a circus band, but now I play happy songs and children dance. My trumpet was my only indulgence through the years. Elgin occasionally speaks silly poems. He once did the odyssey of a gum wrapper, from pulped wood to paper, from printing press to gum stick, from gutter to pulp. It was serio-comic and took a while. These are simple pleasures, but we are fond of them.

This week I think of Jericho, although I am not Joshua. I have walked in this city and waited for walls to tumble. I think some of them just have. With the death of Teeney and the disappearance of Maria a lot that was once abstract comes home. I ruminate on mur-der, and wish to speak straight-out. I'm not just talking about the murder of innocence, but the reality. Jericho has forgotten what is real.

We are familiars of the basic television murder. It happens at the point of a pistol or automatic rifle. Sometimes, in an attempt at realism, the murdered man or woman is flung backward. If the per-son is then seen dying, there is gentle flow of breath and eyes close. Cut to the face of a grief-stricken warrior or widow, sirens rise in the distance, and I, or somebody, appears on the screen and sells soap.

This is not the way of violent murder. In general, when shot by anything more robust than a thirty-eight, the body jerks or twists. There is no grand or artistic arc. The bullet causes a moderate wound on entry, and on exit leaves a hole the size of a dinner.

Eyes either roll to the back of the head, or stare fixedly. It is uncommon when blood and vomit do not saturate shirtfronts or blouses. And it *is* common for murdered people to become spastic, swallow their tongues. The wound is generally ragged, flayed pieces of flesh like windows blown open and red curtains aflutter. Bowels and kidneys discharge, so the corpse is awash in urine and shit. If gut-shot the stench is incredible. The flow of blood from shocked flesh seems unending, but if the wound is sizable and life lingers, it will take only about twenty minutes before the corpse drains. This is the standard murder with a gun.

Teeney, however, was probably not shot. The police have never said how the girls are killed, thus women on the street have no way to guess which wind blows and who to avoid. If murder is by knife, which is probable here, death may come a bit more slowly and with more drama, depending on whether the knife is used to slash or stab. Black men usually slash. White men usually stab. The difference in methods is cultural. A second likely alternative in Teeney's murder is choking, a death incredibly ugly, for eyes displace from sockets. The tongue protrudes in less-than-comic fashion.

I do not try to revulse or entice you, only show in my poor way that we are conned and fleeced each time we buy the standard video murder. There is no beauty in murder, and precious little drama. Even when the "bad-guy sleazebag" gets shot, there's no justice because of the speed of death. Black hats deserve to suffer, or do they? It seems that we who live in Jericho need to come up with better answers.

Some such thoughts occurred to me two evenings ago as I sat with Hal and Symptomatic Nerve Gas. We perched on the top step leading to The Sanctuary. Gray afternoon faded toward gray evening, and the street seemed beautiful. It was the first evening when I felt the dee-rail washed from my system. It is not enough to be sober, merely; one must be in a clarified state to enjoy the senses. I like the taste of fresh rain, but even civilized rain is not bad. It doesn't pick up much auto exhaust in its fall from heaven.

Symptomatic Nerve Gas is not an ignorant man. His mind can wrap easily around an abstraction, but his tongue cannot.

48

"Van Loon's about to eighty-six," he says. "Van Loon's gonna break. When he does, stay way-far-away from the poor s.o.b." Symptomatic Nerve Gas has large hands. The middle knuckle on the right hand is huge and rides slightly behind the alignment of the other knuckles. "Broke when I plowed a guy in New Bedford," he once explained. "Back in '56 at the Wagon Wheel bar. Hell of a name for a New Bedford bar. Ought to of been in Utah."

"I did a schtick in Salt Lake once," I told him. "It could use a few bars. It could use comedians and carousels, but it settles for 2.4 beer and snake oil. Curious sense of humor."

Before Cathedral Mansion Hotel sit three ragged-out Harleys and a Japanese crotch-rocket with a top end of maybe 130. The glory days of bikes are past. You never see the old marques anymore, the Bezas, Triumphs, Ariel Square Fours, Vincents, Norton Manxes. You don't see Velocette Venoms or Phantom Clubmen or The Matchless. Mostly what you see speaks oriental.

"Van Loon has a noble spirit," Hal says. "He has sensibility. I understand his plight." Hal's voice is quiet, his dark, dark eyes attentive to a group of children drawing a hopscotch board on pavement beneath the awning of the truck axle company. Vandermeer's Great Dane is nowhere seen. Probably in its doghouse beneath the old alder. "Van Loon is beset by demons." Hal glances toward the parked bikes. One of the Harleys has a dented gas tank where Van Loon hit it with a ball bat.

Hal's broadsword rises behind his head. Where the sword enters the scabbard Hal wraps a little cloak of plastic warding against moisture. The sword's name is Defender. We have only seen it drawn once. When Hal first came to The Sanctuary, Silk asked to see the sword.

"You're a good kid." Symptomatic Nerve Gas has a deep voice, husky when sounding kind. "Good kids can still have their heads up their keisters." He taps the side of his own head. Then, thinking about it, gives the side of his head a couple of hard smacks. "The demons are here, man," he says. "They're in our own heads. Maria's missing. Katie Van Loon fucks anything that forks a bike, and we just sit and shit." His purpled and fleshy face is both sad and angry. His lips are swollen. All that will reduce that swelling are words he does not have. "Van Loon's goin' over the edge. He'll get a pistol. He's taken one beating. Maybe he's already got a pistol."

49

Hal sits quietly. If it were not for Hal, Van Loon would be in either a hospital or the morgue.

"It was pretty as a picture." Symptomatic Nerve Gas smiles, remembering the fight. He leans back and stares skyward, where darkness works its expanse toward the city. It is Saturday night. Hal will not patrol the plaza. He stays in the neighborhood on weekends.

The fight was not pretty as a picture, unless you like the Dada school of art. The fight was brief and ugly and ridiculous. I tell about the fight only to show what desperate emotions flurry along this wet street.

From a third-floor window of Cathedral Mansion a piece of women's underwear flew like the tawdry flag of some ancient conqueror. It hung tacked to a busted pool cue, the cue wedged between window and frame. No one doubted Katie Van Loon's pants, and no one doubted they hung as challenge to the old man. Van Loon had already threatened one biker. This was the biker's retort: a pair of $1.79 Woolworth drawers.

Van Loon is big. In another time he might have skippered a canal barge in Holland, or stood the bridge of an oceangoing tug. He's a man of commerce, but of action as well. These days he runs a small scrap yard specializing in marine salvage: used binnacles, steering motors, capstans, and copper pipe. He stepped from his small house carrying a ball bat—lucky for the bikers because Van Loon might have carried a wrecking bar—and while the bikers call him "old man" he is in his early forties, and fit. These bikers need cheap taunts. They are punks, not Hell's Angels or Gypsy Jokers. I watched from the steps of The Sanctuary, and Symptomatic Nerve Gas sat beside me. At the time my brain still burned from the after effects of dee-rail.

Even when furious, this Dutchman was methodical. The ball bat seemed a small stick in his large hands. His shoulders were square, his blond hair glowed in the gloom. His feet are curiously small for a large man. He is not normally red-faced, but was on this day. His eyes squinched so small they were piglike. When he arrived before the parked bikes he stood silent for several seconds, deciding which one he would first destroy. He should have brought an axe, because the ball bat broke to flinders on the third stroke. The head of the bat skipped into light traffic, bounced against a bus, skittered back to the curb, a gleaming spot of debris. Van Loon kicked the bike over as four bikers emerged yelling from Cathedral Mansion. They looked like sinewy rabbits, all cock and hop.

Van Loon broke his hand on the first biker's forehead. Even from across the street I could hear bone crunch. The biker's eyes crossed as he stood straight, staggered backward, hit the brick wall of Cathedral Mansion, and slithered to the ground like the wily coyote in a Roadrunner cartoon. Van Loon stood 1 and 0 as the situation deteriorated. He managed to remove a few teeth from a second biker before the other two hit him.

Dada. Dada. Dada. However, matters were becoming serious. Symptomatic Nerve Gas was now on his feet, about to head for the action.

Had it been television, two men would have held the victim while a third man punched the gut. This, however, was not television. The biker with broken teeth went for Van Loon's balls and got a knee for his pains. A second biker clubbed Van Loon beside the head. A third biker pulled a woods knife from his belt. The Great Dane woofed from behind its fence. Traffic churned. Demonic voices chuckled from the tower. Furious movement erupted from stage-right as Hal arrived.

I have never seen a man move so quickly, and my life has been spent around performers. He seemed like the white spirit of wind. Hal finished the fight with three moves. He knocked the knife away, pushed the biker so tidily the man crashed to his butt without getting hands down to break the fall. The biker yelled as Hal kicked feet from beneath a second biker. Then Hal restrained Van Loon. Fade out on a rumpled scene, three bikers on the ground, one with a heavily bruised hip, one out cold, and one staggering to his feet. The man with broken teeth spit blood, dusted his hands in signal of victory, and headed back into Cathedral Mansion, leaving his colleagues to their fates. Hal steered Van Loon home, from which he later departed to get a cast on his hand. Above them all Katie Van Loon's drawers hung momentarily inflated in a light breeze.

"I used to think," Symptomatic Nerve Gas says, "that when you'd seen one swish you'd seen 'em. Look at that." He points to a fat-quack-Cadillac in toenail-pink parked before the homosexual bar. Beside the Cad stands a lean black dude in a pink nighty ornamented everywhere with feathers. The guy wears a costume head resembling a fox. He has a beagle dog on a leash, and though his metaphor be mixed, it is *his* fantasy and he seems proud. His escort is a white guy in silk jacket emblazoned with the picture of a hunting horse jumping fence.

"This is about as deep as we can afford to let it get." Symptomatic Nerve Gas is no longer amused, if he ever was. "We have to quit talkin' and do something."

"What should we do that we're not doing?" I ask. "We search for Maria. We can't put leg irons on Katie. If Van Loon is set to kill a biker some would say he does the Lord's work. . . . " I pause. What I've said is not funny—not to Hal. . . .

"Try shooting somebody," Symptomatic Nerve Gas tells me. "See how you like it."

It is not funny to him, either. Maybe it simply isn't funny. "Van Loon should not suffer the fact of having killed," I say. That is what they want to hear from me, and their wants are correct. These men understand moral absolutes.

Symptomatic Nerve Gas points toward the homosexual bar and the pink Cadillac. "I mean the whole dittybag," he says. "We have to do something about it."

I understand his wants, see no way to satisfy. In the world of cause and effect, that swish and his Cadillac are both cause *and* effect. They are, themselves, symptomatic. Our man, here, with his symptomatic phrases and his command voice, wants to break the cycle. Hopeless task. Playing with words.

"Queers will be queers," I tell him, and it sounds like a homily. "Theirs is a world that says, '*who* you are is *what* you bed.' It's a standard illusion."

"We do not place ourselves at odds with all the world," Hal says, "or those shapes the world portrays. Take care of life and let life run its race. Otherwise you will go mad."

Hal is correct. We at The Sanctuary have dropped away from society, but not from life. It is a new realization for me.

"We have to start sometime, someplace." Symptomatic Nerve Gas watches darkness above the city, and in his eyes lie other darkness. This man has seen the heart and belly of horror. Somehow he prevails. He has seen the blood of thousands, yet he sits before this broken church distraught because a world spits singular violence. I wonder from what obscure place he hails. Probably a farm in Iowa. A country boy who set out to see the world.

"The cops don't give two whoops," he says, and from the moisture in corners of eyes which have seen terrible visions I understand he thinks of Teeney. "It's Maria now, Katie next month." He looks to where children play hopscotch beneath the awning of the truck axle company. They hop in dimmest light. "In three or five years it's one of them."

He's wrong about the police. Some of them probably care. Plus, they have a reputation to uphold.

"We get around," he says. "We go places."

"We are spirits of the street," Hal says. "We walk invisible through crowds. People think us strange, and in their eyes we count for less than naught. We have great advantage."

My heart fills with wonder. Hal has the crux of what Symptomatic Nerve Gas tries to say. We *are* invisible. Nobody watches street people. In addition, invisibility is my specialty.

"We got to stop the bastard." Symptomatic Nerve Gas is set to find a murderer. Does he think himself a detective? Good luck, brother.

On the other hand, why not try? Nothing else works. If the murderer could be found by conventional methods the police would have him by now.

"We can start by looking for a black van," I tell them. "Word has it Maria was seen riding in a black van." I look at Hal. "I'll begin searching tomorrow when I go into role. I'll act a woman's part. Don't be alarmed. Shakespeare used to do it." To Symptomatic Nerve Gas I say, "There's nothing faggy about it."

I stand, headed for bed and sleep. The role will require a lot. It is best to be rested.

VIII

I love to wake early and watch first light etch the room. In this Northwest where my husband and I have spent these many years it sometimes seems the month is always October. At other times it is November or July, never anything else. Spring resembles fall and winter, while winter resembles anything temperate and wet. Season after season I wake this way and sense more than see the dawn. It's habit, formed back when our girls were little, but big enough to sleep the night.

Year after year I wake this way; a habit, but a habit turned into a good and comforting thing. In fact, when a habit becomes comforting we change its name and call it "ritual." Thus we live. Mostly by autumn light.

This year sees my fifty-eighth birthday, Jim's sixtieth, and our thirty-sixth anniversary. The girls, Matthew and Trollop, are about their separate lives; but I still have hopes for them. And, of course, those are my private and nearly endearing names for the kids. Matthew is really named Susan. Trollop is named Judith.

I wake early to enjoy the silence. In those days of growing girls, and when Jim's business fledged, memory gives back pictures of constant activity, squalls, banter, laughter, children's toys. Memory gives pictures of Jim, his head filled with plans and covered with nicely barbered hair. He ruined clothes like a maniac in those days. Made no difference if he wore a business suit, when a truck broke down, or there was some other problem, he would have hands on it before his help had a chance. He seemed happier then, although he seems content now, but memory recalls a laughing and sometimes frustrated man who had too little time and enough worries to keep him going.

These days I wake for other reasons of silence. The city rises soon. It will get snappish and crude. Traffic will cruise from this hill toward downtown. Although our house sits far from the street and behind brick walls, sounds of frustration honk their crazy ways into that Jericho now filled with insurance companies and stockbrokers. It was a simpler and easier city, once, and I mourn its passing.

For, you see, there is something *wrong* with the way we live. I don't like to think about it, avoid thinking about it, but no doubt will do so later because thoughts of what we do return and return. Women, I believe, grow suspicious around make believe.

I wake for silence before Jim stirs. He will step yawning from the bedroom, turn on the television to catch weather reports. His trucks run east and west across mountain passes. There's a lot of snow and ice up there. In deference to me he keeps the television low. It seems a nearly apologetic presence in the house, but it reminds me of the temptation of Eve. I was brought up religious, can't help thinking that way. That unfortunate Eve had only to put up with forbidden fruit, while we Eves of an older and less innocent time are obligated not to temptation, but to rename necessity. In a fanciful way one might say I have an electronic serpent in my living room. I remind myself I was not born and raised to be a shopper. It is different with my daughters. Matthew shops careers. Trollop shops men.

*   *   *

No role I've ever taken has come toward me so quickly. This woman seems so much myself, speaking from my own heart, I'm not sure I am her or she is me. I can see her husband's shoulders as they hunch above morning coffee and newspaper. I can feel the texture of carpets in her house, can see favorite or loved objects: a figurine once belonging to her mother, or her grandmother's darning egg. This is what I love about theater.

Because I must confess (and other actors will confess this as well) I first became an actor because I did not *like* who I was. An actor can be anyone, the roles changing in the genius of creative energy and imagination. We are sirens and vixens, Tammany bosses, riverboat captains, cowboys, and statesmen. We can be a duchess or Joan of Arc. We hail from the fast track of Manhattan, from Chicago's South Side, or from mist-ridden and deer-breeding hills of Wyoming sunrises. An actor can be anyone, and I can be her, with her joys and sorrows and memories.

I do know one thing. This week we are on the street. Today Silk promises to help with the role. Silk and I will poke our noses into a few shops, then lunch. After that I am off to my duty. This is my week to help run the thrift store sponsored by her—no—my church. Women of our congregation divide the duty. The store is open Monday through Saturday. Maybe we do some good.

Makeup takes time. I sit among depilatories. My breasts were never big. They say we change as we age. More of our hormones are getting their thoughts mixed up. Men grow rudimentary breasts and women shrink. I pinch mine, rub them, and the body comes alive and feminine. Sex was a problem when we first married, largely because Jim had no more experience than I. Then sex became routine. Now it is gentle and there's some substance to it. I'll never understand what drives Trollop. Her needs seem to have something to do with the way she feels about herself.

If there's substance to sex, there is also substance to nylon that no man knows—unless, perhaps—he parachutes. Silk has wonderful legs. We'll be quite a pair. We'll turn the eyes and thoughts of

57

handsome men. Mature, handsome men. We'll joke about it, and that's the best reason to do it.

No. This is not the way this woman thinks. With sex she would not be explicit. At best she might remember a time when Silk walked past and men's heads turned. She would not admire her own legs, would not think of them. I'm still projecting into the role. Try again.

The street today seems calm. Silk and I bus to town. Commuters have already commuted, their cars rest in high-rise parking lots of gray concrete. Skyscrapers cast crashed masts of shadows. Mixed clouds with watery sun attempt mild blessing on this city, and I feel a bit courageous. Twice during the past year drive-by shootings occurred downtown. Five bystanders wounded, a seventeen-year-old drug dealer killed. Silk and I do not enter a war zone, but a zone where war can happen.

I only understand a little about a world in which a seventeen-year-old lies dead at the hands of seventeen-year-olds with automatic weapons. It is not enough to say I do not understand drugs. It is not enough to say some people should not be parents. These are things my friends say, and for the most part they are sincerely said. The questions are too important and too complicated. One may simply not dismiss them. Still, if I have some understanding, it probably does nothing in the balance of things.

Horror rises from history. I've lived long enough to know that.

"That man over there," Silk whispers, "led a glamorous early life. He was a secret cowboy and noted cattle rustler. Now he is a microbiologist who lives alone with a horse named Howard and a bacteria named George." Silk delivers this with a straight face, and I giggle. It is a game we play, making up imagined careers for people who seem to need them. The man she gifts so eloquently must surely be a lawyer who prepares briefs but does not try cases. Nicely dressed, too mousy for a courtroom.

Silk dresses with great care, always. Today she wears those

shades of gray and green which spell wealth. Her skirt is fashionable in Boston, below the knee and above the calf; simply cut and in fashion everywhere at times, but always in Boston. Her blouse is understated gray, her cloth coat matching the green skirt. She wears low heels, her hair is coiled.

"The lady over there," I say, "is curator of an art museum. She sometimes buys marginal work from promising artists. She takes those chances so they will not starve." The lady in question has jowls. Her print dress is orange and purple. She wears purple heels. Her scowl is critical, but probably not of art.

We ride and watch. When the bus stops for passengers we search second- and third-floor apartment windows, or survey benches in the small parks of this city. Both of us look for Maria, but neither says anything.

Riding beside Silk the old devil of history once more rises. I tried to raise my children correctly, perhaps I shielded them. I remember a time when my family may have been right, or maybe wrong. It was 1936, and our congregation buried its preacher. I was six years old.

His name was Minimon or Minimin, something dangerously close to "minimum," and he had the small Lutheran parish in Hartford City, Indiana. I imagine him a good, small-town preacher of his day; for how much of a child's mind is able to lay subtle weights? As a child the world fills with darkness and light, utter absolutes. He once preached that the Great Depression was a visitation of God on America for the sins of the Roaring Twenties. The man must have had some historical sense.

We were not shielded from death in those days. Death was not a television show. In a grim way an important funeral became a social occasion. The Reverend Mr. Minimon died Sunday night and could not be buried until Saturday, because work went on in the fields. The dead were kept above ground for long periods in those days. They were fully mourned, not cremated in tidy silence. Our preacher lay in state in the parsonage for six days of June heat.

In those days the community was the family, and the family

the community. Even today, in that small Indiana town, perhaps a third or fourth of the people are my distant relations. I recall my grandmother's grim remark that "Other people [and perhaps she meant Baptists or perhaps she meant Missouri Synod Lutherans] could hold a circus when they buried, but we knew how to do a funeral right." She took pride in our stateliness; stiff upper lips, formality precise as furrows running in the fields. Grandma loved the men's dark wool suits, their cereal-bowl haircuts, tightly knotted ties. Such things spoke discipline and form. We girls were starchy in our gray and black dresses, with starchy lace. Even in the Great Depression starch was easy come by.

To this day flowers alarm me, unless I anticipate them. When the girls were born Jim sent flowers to the hospital. On wedding anniversaries roses arrive. Such flowers do not bode ill. It is the occasional appearance. If we have friends for dinner I must anticipate, for often these days people bring flowers instead of wine. Or flowers may suddenly appear in restaurants, on cosmetic counters, or in hotel rooms when we vacation. After fifty-two years the flower messages remain frightening echoes.

Think of the mind of a six-year-old, sleepy or impatient during sermons. Think of the world as yet unfolded, the magic of stories told in evenings, the even more remarkable magic of sunrises and birds, of redhaws or apricots coloring trees. At six almost anything can be a first experience.

The Reverend Mr. Minimon was in first stages of physical decay, although I have no doubt his soul stood with God. He lay in an ebony coffin on the sun porch of the parsonage. Flowers ranked the coffin, stood on tables, and huge funerary baskets stood on the floor. Viewers walked between small forests of flowers, and six-year-olds walked among flowers standing high as their shoulders. The congregated flowers were heavy with scent, and even the flowers—at least some that arrived early—were in decay.

Children were required to climb on a two-step dais so we might say good-bye to our preacher. The Reverend Mr. Minimon was sculpted wax. The mouth did not move, his crossed hands seemed curiously folded blades with no demarcation between stubby fingers. The child's mind could not connect this wax with the tall and darkly dressed man who stood at the portal after services shaking hands, even with older children. Would the Reverend Mr. Minimon have wanted this forced farewell by children?

The sweet smell of beginning decay was not exactly new to me, for children find dead birds and mice. What was new was the association between death and flowers. Beginning terror made me tremble. I thought of those bladelike hands reaching from the coffin to shake my hands. As I stood on the dais my father held my arm so I would not tip forward toward the coffin. Because he held me I understood that I might tip forward. My father was never an easy man to be around, but I have always carefully loved him for his attempt at consideration. Terror in the young is no less because one is young. Terror is terror.

"I worry about Hal," Silk says. "His delusion doesn't fade."

We are at lunch in the tearoom of this city's best department store. It is nice to rest. Shopping is a young woman's game. I wanted to gift Silk with a new outfit, because she wears only cast-offs. They are sometimes designer cast-offs, but cast-offs nonetheless. She instead chose a small Indian carving in stone.

Ladies sit in twos and threes at tables ornate in cloth and silver. Waitresses and a few busboys drift through the large room. Luncheons appear from wheeled carts. Silk looks the finest lady here, although I doubt she owns as much coin as can be found in the average poor box. Her years in convent, with vows of chastity and poverty, prepared her for a life of the spirit. Her face still reflects holy light. When she speaks of Hal I hear gentle wistfulness of a woman who has given birth, raised and launched the child, and now seeks memories of days when all things yet seemed possible.

61

"Our own delusions do not fade, either," I say. "The kids dash around in confusion. We continue to think our hope will breed good facts. Hal plays on his own stage."

"Things add up," Silk tells me. "Hal's becoming like a son. I hoped for children."

Teacups click like muted exclamation points. Murmured conversations about dress and men and kids and college are subdued like soft light.

"There's a difference between delusion and fooling yourself. I fool myself until it's time to do something else." Silk still wears her wedding ring. Her hands are firm and capable. That delicate face with gray eyes is not beyond a tremor around the lips. Silk buries her emotions deep.

"I didn't want to love anyone again." Silk murmurs this, as much to herself as to me. "I do not fear pain, or don't fear it so awful much. It's the way things add up. I'm trying to do my bit." Silk lives in The Sanctuary surrounded by men. Perhaps she has no real women friends. She might have spoken her private heart long before had she another woman to confide in.

Three tables away a pair of transvestites attempt to pass as respectable women. They have doubtless planned this downtown sortie for weeks. One can imagine them joking, saying the whole business is droll if it can be pulled off. What a shocker for the Yankee ladies.

One of the men is short and chubby, dressed in yellow frock far too young for him. The other is slender, his boyish face beneath blond wig sports too much makeup. We all pretend this is not happening. The management is doubtless embarrassed. The transvestites speak too quickly, and it's obvious, even to them, most people in the room have tumbled to their act.

"What do you worry about?" I ask Silk. "You can't protect Hal, and I've only just been thinking we protect the kids in dangerous ways. When nothing bad ever happens they don't guard themselves." I think of the seventeen-year-old drug dealer dead before gunfire. I think of Maria, of Teeney. Teeney never thought she would die.

"I worry about three things. Hal is young and strong. In an ancient sense Hal is virtuous." Silk sees my objection, and answers before I can say anything. "Hal is fearless. Sooner or later he will get in a situation where he feels called to use that weapon. If it happens later, it will be because he ages. There will be a time when his agility and strength begin to fade. If he is forced to use that weapon he's doomed."

Three tables away the restaurant manager attempts to get rid of the transvestites. There is not much he can do as long as they cause no disturbance. If he makes them leave they'll sue. Some ladies already clutch their purses, preparing to depart. For them, a day of shopping and lunch lies in ruins. The ladies seem offended in the same way a man is offended when he is not allowed to do his work.

"It means jail or a sanitarium if he uses the sword," I say. "He's not the man to use it. It's never drawn."

"Hal can stand jail," Silk says. "But he is gentle and a gentleman. If he uses that weapon his great punishment will be his conscience. He'll be unable to live."

What Silk says makes sense. Men like Hal bedevil themselves with their mistakes. They rarely give themselves credit for their goodness. Women are more practical.

"I have two other fears," Silk says. "If I love Hal, and Hal is destroyed, I will be in despair. That would be wrong." Her voice changes, so she seems almost a lecturer. When Silk was in convent, was she a teaching nun?

"There is a weight of joy and a weight of despair running in the world," she tells me. "Every little piece of despair adds up. I don't want to contribute despair. It's my obligation to the world."

And so this is why she loves small things only. Belov'ed Silk. Dear, dear Silk. What kind of conscience do they give you in convent?

The transvestites arrive at their big moment of surprise. As the restaurant manager stands watching, they rise and remove their wigs. The stocky one seems jolly and without malice. The boy, however, looks vicious. The two men bow to the remaining ladies. A seventeen-year-old girl, sitting beside her grandmother and her aunt, makes an obscene gesture. Waves of silent shock follow the gesture. The girl is small, skinny, red-faced with anger. The transvestites bow again, then giggle. The seventeen-year-old is furious. She seems about to throw a heavy silver teapot. I am stunned. Perhaps no place is safe these days, even this teashop once safe as a vault.

Silk watches the young girl. Silk is every bit as confused as the rest of us.

"I worry over one other thing," Silk says. "Hal recognizes demons. He doesn't understand that you can't fight evil, only assert good. When you fight, as that young girl is fighting, the damage happens in your own soul." Silk says this, but her eyes hold questions. "I think that's true."

"There is right and there is wrong," I tell her, "but it's getting harder to tell which is which."

"Evil is not the absence of good. Evil is an independent force. Demons are real." Silk arranges her napkin and prepares to leave. Her lecturing voice passes. Now her voice holds just a hint of fear. "Hope is so frightening," she tells me. "I still search for Maria, but hope comes and goes."

I settle our check and we leave the teashop. The escalator is busier than usual, as ladies leave in disgust. I do not know what happens to the two men. Silk and I ride to the main floor.

A phantasmic display of designer jeans and cosmetics stands ranked by five television monitors showing a discreet rock video. I wonder how such a thing can be discreet. It seems a contradiction. The colors are washed in the monitors. Something wrong in the transcription. The volume is low. Young women sit before mirrored tables, and saleswomen encourage them toward this cosmetic or that.

We step onto the street and Silk pauses to thank me. Her thanks are sincere, so she need say little, and nothing effusive. I watch her walk away. She keeps one hand in her coat pocket. She runs her fingers across a small stone sculpture. I know she is happy as well as pleased. The sculpture will not change, and it will not fade.

IX

The street seems filled with danger. Traffic passes, but no black vans appear. The vans which pass carry commercial decorations, florists, auto parts, delivery services. Signs on vans carry pictures of speedy cartoon characters, smiling chipmunks delivering balloons. Sometimes it seems the entire world is a logo.

The thrift shop where I work is in long walking distance. It would take five minutes by cab, thirty-five on a circuitous bus ride. The walk will do me good, and danger is mostly imaginary. Beggars queue up around department stores. They are a big problem these days, and they are my personal problem. My husband no longer comes downtown. Beggars make him angry, and anger is bad for his heart. I do not know what I'll do when Jim is taken from me. These days, more than ever, I fear being alone.

Jim does not get angry at street musicians or cripples. He becomes furious when approached by younger men. Such men often sit with cardboard signs: "Help me get back to Kansas," "No job, three kids," "I'm not a drunk." Jim will sometimes give a dollar to a drunk. He had his own bout with drinking years ago. "There's always hope for a drunk," he says, and I wonder if he tries to buy redemption. His life has not been easy.

We are children of the Great Depression, Jim and I. We watched a system fail. Failure lived all around us. Fear lived in the eyes of our fathers, and in the voices of our mothers. We grew with such fear of failure that it was almost impossible for us to fail.

Symptomatic Nerve Gas stands on a corner beneath the plastic sign of a bank, and before a cash machine. His appearance nearly takes me out of role. Today, Symptomatic Nerve Gas roars, "Felony Assault!" To emphasize his act, he wears a Halloween mask of a skull. Somewhere he has obtained an array of political campaign buttons, the buttons covering the front and arms of his shirt: Nixon — Ford — Kennedy — Eisenhower — Reagan — Bush — also buttons of congressmen and port commissioners. Symptomatic Nerve Gas stands beside a hand-lettered sign, and holds a second sign high above the crowd. The sign he holds displays a small photo of Maria Ramirez. It reads: "Have you seen this girl? Big reward."

What reward can any of us offer? I'm the only one with lots of money, and I don't care for it. All I use it for is food and props. That's the only reward we could come up with.

The sign sitting beside Symptomatic Nerve Gas is elaborate. He is sometimes remarkable in his productions. This sign carries clipped newspaper photos of all the murdered girls. Three corpses remain unidentified, and the sign shows three skulls and question marks. At the bottom of the sign is a blank space, lettered below: "Who Is Next? Your Daughter?" Symptomatic Nerve Gas does not understand that scare advertising is the last resort of the commercially down-and-out.

I walk past the signs. On the sidewalk a woman sits with her two children. This woman is different from the rest. I nearly leap past hoping she does not raise her eyes. She may recognize me. She is the daughter of someone, from somewhere, sometime. I do not recall her name. A brown-haired daughter. Tennis lessons. Good grades. Her children sit wrapped in blankets once bought at a fine store, and this morning stripped from a bed. Before her sits a small box of origami cranes, and a sign pricing them at fifty cents. I imagine her going to a dime store, buying the origami paper—red—blue—green—purple—spending a desolate evening folding the cranes; a skill learned in Girl Scouts or maybe art school. Half a lifetime and two children, her only salable product tiny folded birds from a civilization and artform she does not understand.

This is going too far. There is something *wrong* with the way we live. I am not sure I can bear this. Take a few deep breaths. Grandmother was right about a lot of things. Formality, stiff upper lip, carry on. We do not behave like Baptists.

What to do? Approach her? Her shame would be too great. On the other hand she has children. Shame weighs not less, but differently.

How down on her luck can anyone become? I know the answer. We children of the Great Depression know how bad things can get, and how quickly they can get that way.

This is shocking. Shocking. I stand at an intersection. A red, white, and blue directional sign points the route to a freeway.

I can rescue her now. Take her home. Jim will understand. Children in the house for a day or two. A job with Jim's company, or with the company of some friend. Has her husband deserted? Is there a divorce? Is she punishing some man by sitting here on the street? Our young ones sometimes play ugly games. Watery sun glosses the freeway sign.

One child is school-age, the other no more than three. In some nebulous way they must know something awful happens. Memories of childhood assail me. I once saw submission on my father's face. It is wrong to remember such things. Beside me one of those long, ugly limousines swings like a lever, crosses lanes heading for the freeway. My mind follows it, as my body stands beneath the freeway sign. The actor is again watching the actor, not only in role, but in context:

* * *

Freeways extend north and south from Oregon to Canada, carrying overloads of tractor-trailers, buses, camper trucks, and endless streams of autos. Freeways run between great mountain chains, the Olympics to the west, Cascades to the east. Above the chains stand ancient volcanoes, Mount St. Helens, Mount Rainier, Mount Baker. The volcanoes bear permanent glaciers. Freezing mist called whiteouts sail on their peaks. These are sacred mountains above a land now turned profane. Indians used to worship here. Now Indians sometimes hesitate in the hurry and scurry of pedestrian traffic to stand silent and amazed. The mountain ranges are ten million years old, not volcanic but tectonic; folding plates of earth's crust crumpled. The volcanoes stand twelve thousand feet above a city proud of its skyline.

Elgin sits on the steps of The Sanctuary viewing the street. Mixed clouds and sun flatten his dark face, while his broad nose sniffs the air, then sniffs a delicacy. When Silk returned from lunch she brought a small cake wrapped in a napkin. Elgin takes as much joy from smelling the treasure as he will from eating. He sits passive and sleepy in the sun. He has been up all night searching.

On the docks Maria's father, Jorge, loads cartons of supplies into an open workboat. Together with two other men he will ride into anchorage where an oil tanker swings in ballast. These supplies, ham and caviar and strawberries, go to the wardroom. They are a ship chandler's gift to the ship's captain for placing his company's business in the right hands. Jorge moves with smooth, deliberate pace, while the men beside him move faster. There is no flow in their movements. Their actions are ragged and waste energy. Jorge tries to lose himself in the work, tries not to think, and vaguely fights against fatalism that is his nature.

In early afternoon Hal walks in parks. This afternoon he stands near a playground watching baby-sitters and young mothers attend children. On this day of mixed sun there are a lot of them. Older children are in school. This is an outdoor nursery, small bairns tumbling and shouting joy. Hal murmurs thanks to the Blessed Virgin, and doubtless she hears.

Katie Van Loon sits alone in her room. Her mouth holds a pout that sometimes changes to a hiss. Loud music fills the room, and Katie, who is confined, pauses to smack a windowsill to the beat of electronic music. She has no suitcase, but she has a father who she knows, knows nothing. If he knew anything, she would be at school right now. She does not think that she would be cutting school right now.

Rebellion plays through many layers of action, but training also dictates. Katie packs two pillowcases as she prepares to run away. She does this most properly. Blue jeans neatly folded, a small stuffed rabbit named Muffin, underwear, tapes for her boombox, towel, socks, photos of her little brother, an extra pair of shoes. Katie looks in a mirror. Her face seems fine. She does not see young frustration which demands that music must always play; for if the music ever stops there will be no one at home behind those eyes. Her lips show that she has never been happy for more than fifteen consecutive minutes. It is very, very hard to be young.

The city hums. This is not a busy hive. It more resembles schematics for a computer; traffic lights are gates, and cars swing right or left like electronic impulses. Traffic covers the street, as the street leads to the freeway.

On a corner beside a sign pointing to a freeway, a handsome Yankee lady searches her purse. She finds an envelope containing bills she will pay. She places the bills back in her purse. It is the envelope she wants. The lady takes cash from her purse and puts it in the envelope, quite a lot of cash. Then, in an action still possible in the Northwest, she approaches an elderly gentleman who wears a tailored suit. The lady explains what she wants, quietly indicates a young woman and two children who sit on the sidewalk half a block away. The gentleman nods. He takes the envelope, adds money of his own, walks toward the destitute woman. He bends down, picks an origami crane from a small box, and leaves the envelope.

In the north end of the city a large parking lot holds what seems shiploads of cars. This is a park-and-ride lot, a place for commuters to leave cars as they bus to town. Cars here are standard, mostly Japanese rice grinders, a few small Fords and Chevies. The cars look like patchwork, but here and there a vehicle is remarkable—a working pickup, or a dump truck, or a Yankee's Continental. The expensive vehicles call attention to themselves. They are first to suffer break-ins from thieves who prowl this lot.

A black van sits impenetrable as a safe. It is ornamented with painted demons; and although thieves have tried to crack it they've had no luck. This van has no alarm system. It carries a revenge system. Touch it and you serve as ground for 12-volt current.

Traffic pounds. Cars pass parks, wooded ravines, vacant lots, and hillsides too steep for houses. Pockets of wildness still exist in this city. Trees stand everywhere, for, in perpetual rain, trees grow like weeds. Wild roses twine among wild blackberries in every place inaccessible to bulldozers. Even now, as traffic runs the freeways like an iron along its board, deer live in ravines while raccoons pilfer from garbage cans. This is the Western Flyway, thus ducks, geese, scoters, grebes, an occasional sea harrier. Squirrels are not an endangered species here, nor are rabbits. Sea lions congregate before fish ladders. All around, life scurries and breeds, and, beside the boom of traffic, also dies.

The naked body of a young woman lies moldering beneath brush on a wooded hillside. The state of decay takes all elasticity from the body which approaches putridity. In a park near a fire station a young man lies beaten. This corpse will soon be found. Bruises do not cover track marks on the arms. An eleven-year-old girl lies stuffed beneath trash in a dumpster. These are the murdered of the central city.

In the north end a clothed corpse, this one female, lies hidden in a half-collapsed garage of an abandoned house. The body is shielded from view by the hulk of a junked car that no longer has an engine. This corpse doubtless arrives here because of a domestic dispute. The corpse was obviously pregnant.

On the east side of the city an old woman's corpse lies on the floor of her small living room. She is dead from a cruel beating. The skull is crushed.

In the south end Maria Ramirez lies hidden in a stand of young fir. Her clothing is in disarray. She is cast-off, obsolete, yesterday's gotta-have-it item and today's refuse. Her dark eyes are fixed, seem startled. There is a wide knife wound in the sternum, and the lower body is mutilated, dark with blood. The best that can be hoped is that the wound in the sternum was the first wound. It would have killed immediately. There are no ribbons ornamenting Maria. She has not been dead for many hours.

This completes this day's inventory of the murdered, a day which, for this city, is about average.

X

At my right hand a Black Forest bear carved from black oak stands on a counter among carnival glass, small pieces of pewter, and a Limoges plate with a chip on its edge. The bear is three feet tall, and gazes with painted eyes at the inside of the thrift shop. Among the ragtag and clutter arriving in this place an occasional piece is deemed "antique." This carving, dated 1836, waits an indiscriminate collector, or an interior decorator.

The carving holds little interest, but I like to think of the man who did the work. I see him sitting at his fireplace with wife and children through a long German winter. His mother and father also lived with him. They were old. They helped raise the children, and they told stories. The children grew to adulthood knowing who they were, where they came from; knew the name of every relative for at least four generations. Not much changed in ways of living from 1836 to 1936. I could once tell what lineal tracings produced a great aunt, or a third cousin twice removed.

That same experience is shared by all who work here. These ladies from my church are old. They come to this thrift shop the way their dead husbands once went to jobs. These women are lonely. The thrift shop gives contact with strangers. They volunteer, year after year, lone souls doing church work in behalf of their sanity. I shudder, fearing I may end this way; among used refrigerators, cast-off clothing, ashtrays stolen from hotels in Reno and Ketchikan.

On the other hand, there is beauty in things well used. A new thing has no history. It has not proved itself.

This afternoon I watch through windows at the street. A drunken man wearing a red felt hat staggers past. Maria will not be found. Symptomatic Nerve Gas is right. We must discover who does the killings and stop him. Silk is right. Hal must never use that weapon. Hal and Elgin may be right. There are such things as demons.

An old woman pushes a shopping cart past the front windows. She does this every day about this time. Ladies in the thrift shop whisper that she is a rich eccentric who collects from trash bins. I've heard the story so often it almost seems true, but isn't. We somehow still believe in magic. We wish to believe young men striding by with brisk movements and electric eyes are filled with purpose. We pretend young girls walk together and giggle, in hopes of Prince Charming. We pretend these things, while around us lies the spindrift of our worlds.

Racks of used clothing cover half the floor space. Polyester and tweed, cotton, wool, many-colored raiment. Actors find costumes here. Artists find work clothes. In a couple of weeks the racks will be raided as people prepare their outfits for Mardi Gras—in this city called Fat Tuesday, and in this year on February fifteenth. These racks of clothing also allow respectable folk inexpensive ways to preserve respectability. Of all our customers, I like the artists best. They know they live off the effluvia of civilization. Men like my husband produce a lot, the artists live on leftovers. Is that right or wrong?

There is so much *stuff* in the world. When one thinks she has seen every single *thing* there is, something appears. In today's contributions the item for whispering is an inflatable and apparently usable penis. It can be deflated, rolled, and carried in a purse. The ladies utter horrified whispers, throw the thing in the trash. We all suppose it from Japan, or at least Taiwan. Orientals, the ladies agree, are like rabbits.

Two aisles of kitchen appliances and glassware stand next to the clothing. It seems civilization is bent on uttering saucers. Cups get broken. Saucers remain. After saucers come electric irons, scratches on bottoms, or plastic fabric melted to them like glue. There are MixMasters, plaster gimcracks for the walls with sayings "God Bless Our Home," decals on glasses, worn picnic baskets. On the next aisle sit assortments of tools, parts for cars long in the scrap yard, bolts and chain and a rumple of hardware. Next to these sit furniture, mostly patio tables and televisions this time of year. In autumn, patios are swept with rain. Football season begins. People buy new televisions.

A row of seven televisions mutters on lowest volume, and an actor takes us seven times along a row of produce. The term "actor" is generic. This one is female.

I know this woman. She has worked for the same grocery chain for many years. She sells apples and flank steak, or specials on cheese and peanut butter.

I've known her for years. When we were young we struggled together, fighting for footholds in legitimate theater. She was a brilliant comic, a passable tragedian. Seeing her this way is almost more than I can bear. . . .

. . . I am a dweller among shadows, a keeper of sacred flame. Neon and plastic I watch, also the unfogginess of thermopane. From the belltower of The Sanctuary . . .

*   *   *

Sadness nearly takes me out of role. I will stay away from the televisions, will do God's work among the clothing. Maybe a poor woman with children needs a kindly word.

If there is something wrong with the way we live, my daughters are colorful examples. They never expect hardship. Matthew—no, her name is Susan—will keep her husband scrambling for as long as he puts up with her. Susan takes her self-importance from occupations, and her occupations are defined by her tools. She has been weaver, potter, cabin builder, basketmaker, clothing designer, artist, poet, reupholsterer. She is talented, gains enough skill to produce average work. When she must extend toward mastering difficult details, she chooses another occupation. Her house is a rampage of dusty looms, potters' wheels, quilting frames. Her husband may very likely be a saint.

Judith—the one I nickname Trollop—now enters her fourth divorce. She has been lucky with men. She gets good ones. She also gets bored. While Susan cannot stick with the demands of an occupation, Judith cannot stick with the demands of marriage. She stays with a man until she finds another who will marry her.

Disposable work and disposable marriage. Disposable people. Our possessions used to teach us how to use them.

A tall woman lingers among the clothing racks. There is something unsettling about her, a sort of indifferent contempt. She stands near, and dwarfs, a Korean mother, grandmother, and baby. On the sidewalk two young men exchange money and drugs. They are not even looking around for the police. I saw fifty such events from this store before understanding what was happening. A black man and a white man shamble past, raise voices to each other. They tell of their experiences, and both are drunk.

This tall woman has the wrong hand movements. Women are raised to know finite movements. They know what fabric will do, and they may jerk at it but will not tear at it. They lift fabric, don't simply pick it up. Fabric to a woman is the same as lumber to a man. It demands correct use.

Something is wrong here. This woman certainly looks like a woman, though strangely dressed. I judge her age at early thirties, her clothing appropriate for a prostitute or a seventeen-year-old. Her skirt is tight as second skin, cut three inches above the knee. It is black rayon, her blouse is dimestore peach. The blouse has half sleeves with imitation lace in royal purple. It is cut low enough to display tops of her breasts. Her shoes are patent leather, three-inch heels. Those long legs seem spindly. At the same time they are muscular, like those of a runner or a tennis player. I look at her knowing what my husband would say. Jim would say, "It pays to advertise."

What is wrong? Her hair is dusty blond. The hair falls loose nearly to the middle of her back. Her hair is luxuriant, a denial of the cheapness of her outfit. She has a nice forehead, an astoundingly good nose. It is not Roman, but is the central feature of her face. Her lips are thin, pursed above material.

Her wrists seem too large for her arms. Maybe she works in a fish cannery; but that can't be true. Long fingernails, almost wickedly long, glow iridescent violet, and her eyes are violet blue. Her shoulders are not heavy, but her hands are wide, almost square. She has selected a badly worn black silk blouse, also a worn half-slip in black.

Terror grips me as if I were a small girl gazing into a coffin. These completely useless garments could be cut into streamers. They could be black ribbons.

That's insane. I've been too preoccupied remembering Teeney, searching for Maria. I'm starting to see murderers everywhere, even in the pathetic shape of a tasteless and ignorant woman who probably holds a bad job. This is crazy.

On the other hand maybe it isn't crazy. If the murderer has not been caught these several years it's because he is—or she is—smart. The murderer would not go to stores and buy black ribbons. The murderer would haunt the thrift stores where runaway girls find cheap coats.

My terror is real. If someone showed me flowers right now I

would scream. The mind sometimes *knows* what the mind rejects. I want to flee, want my home, my life, the comfort of familiar things. Will anyone care about Grandmother's darning egg when I am dead?

I want my husband. I want the past. I don't care if we were poor. I don't want this. I don't want murder and drugs and memories of a waxen corpse. Jim and I worked so hard. We struggled. We did it the way we were supposed to, in the eyes of God and the eyes of man. What has gone wrong?

The woman selects a third garment, sleazy and black, one of those nightgowns made only to take off. She actually holds it before her, and rubs it against the inside of her leg. She drifts toward the counter at the front of the store. As she pays her dollar she chats with the lady at the counter. The lady takes the dollar, stuffs the purchases in a paper grocery bag. The lady seems both puzzled and hostile. She attempts to be courteous, but has lived too long and been Lutheran too long. She barely avoids rudeness.

I don't want to follow this woman. Fears flash through my mind. It seems I follow death itself. At the same time we must know our enemy. Duty insists on courage. As I pass the front counter I tell the lady I'll be back in a few moments. A short errand. The lady mutters something about perverts.

Once on the sidewalk I'm unsure how to act. On television the police are skilled in following people. The problem with television is that the people who are followed are always in a hurry. How do you follow someone who stops before shopwindows, who gives quarters to beggars, who has no particular destination? I stand and stare. That's the wrong way, but the woman does not seem to notice.

The woman stands before a drunken man who sits in the entry of an empty store front. She murmurs to him, searches her purse, gives two dollars.

"Momma, you so good," the man says. "You *look* so good, you crazy momma." The man struggles to his feet. He wears two topcoats, baggy trousers, a red lumberjack shirt, and a soiled red hat.

He hides the money in the pocket of the inner coat. The woman murmurs.

"Sho," the man says, "I tell her. Count on it double. She a good girl."

A message is being passed. I do not know why this woman I follow, and the drunken man, would have anything to do with each other. I do not even know whether to keep following the woman, or follow the drunken man. Maybe he takes a message to a young girl.

How could the killer be a woman, anyway? None of this makes sense, but I think of those muscular legs running, of those square hands hurting someone. I will follow the woman, although this whole business must be some insane fantasy.

We wander along. The woman loiters before a pawnshop where a display of knives is softened by several musical instruments. A trumpet hangs from a wire, an accordion lies in an open case. She hesitates before the doorway of a cheap bar, and I'm afraid she will enter. From the bar comes harsh cursing, also the hoot and jingle of a pinball. The woman moves on.

As we walk, the street gets seamier. Now we pass bookstores loaded with pornography, and walk a long block before a huge building that stands boarded, slated to be torn down. People in sleeping bags lie tucked against the building, while other people wait for buses. This is the spot where the seventeen-year-old was killed in the drive-by shooting. Men stand around in small groups. They talk and laugh. None of the people are well dressed. It may be a killer walks among them, but maybe they are used to that. I follow the woman, listen to cat calls and ugly suggestions as some of the men watch the way she is dressed. They do not look at me, but at my purse. If Jim knew I was in this part of town he would be angry with worry.

Elgin stands on a street corner and appears half asleep. He watches the crowd through drooping eyelids, and his lips move as he makes images. He looks for Maria, still has hope, or maybe his nose sniffs for her in the crowd. As we pass, an image whispers after us, "Teenie giggle, like the alter ego of an inner tear."

I wish Elgin would follow, and probably he does. It is not a good idea to turn around, or show fear. These men can have the purse. It's the grasp and shove and running that would happen. That's what makes me so afraid.

The woman turns a corner and walks toward safer territory. This city has a public market with hundreds of shops selling produce, fish, clothing, crafts. One feels safer. This is a normal place to shop.

Even murderers have to eat. Her errand takes her first among produce. She buys ordinary things, lettuce and an apple. She pauses long enough to buy a fish. She buys a loaf of bread, and then a shopping bag. The very commonness of her acts convinces me my imagination makes me a fool.

The crowd is heavy today. I smell sweat and the rich odor of pipe tobacco. I smell perfume, bath oils, hot chowder. The crowd presses, and the feeling of safety is reassuring. The woman buys coffee beans, then moves almost leisurely around a corner to a walkway leading to a lower level of the market. When I turn the corner she is gone.

I stand confused. All of this has been for nothing. I've left the thrift store where I promised to work. I promised to be gone for only a moment. All of this has come to nothing. All I've done is watch a woman shop. A person can't help feeling ashamed, she can't help wondering why she makes something so normal into something awful. Maybe that woman *likes* to wear black underthings.

"Don't try to turn around." A hand grasps my shoulder, so hard I can feel bruises form. "A rich cunt in the wrong place," the voice says. "Don't let me see you here again." Fingers tighten. No one is this strong. My shoulder feels grasped by a machine. There is nothing I can say. I nod. I am no longer simply suspicious. This *is* the murderer.

The grip relaxes, but it is still firm. I search for tones in the voice. It's not a woman's voice. It's too high-pitched for a man. "When I turn you loose," the voice says, "you stand here. Think ugly. Think what shit will happen. Think about a knife in your asshole. Don't even wiggle for ten minutes." The hand is gone. I stand.

My father once showed submission. We went to a drugstore to get baby food for my newborn brother. My father was three cents short. He begged. I was only three years old. How you can you remember anything that happened when you were three? My father begged.

Crowds pass. Tears from pain come flooding, and I find tissue in my purse. The shock of pain makes me weak, the fear of moving makes me weaker. I lean against a concrete column. People pass, see me wipe my eyes, and cast their gazes down. A shopwindow across the walkway displays a hundred different kinds of colored kites. Some are shaped like fish, or animals, and some are shaped like kites. The wind always blows around here.

"My nose was smelling trouble," Elgin says. He stands beside me gentle as a smile. "I just be thankful Hal was not around. He would have bought some trouble."

Of all things terrible my mind feeds me the Great Depression. We were so poor. Everybody was so poor. My parents were afraid. My mother baked pies and sold them whole for thirty cents.

"It's gone," Elgin says. "Headed for a bus stop."

One thing is certain. This role is finished. The murderer has seen this woman. The murderer knows where she works. I tremble, because it is one thing to be taken out of role, quite another when the role is murdered. I feel her mind screaming, feel her soul draining into darkness.

Is this how death will be? This scream of incredulity, this dark slide of the soul into night? My tears will not stop, but now they are for her. My shoulder feels dislocated. The pain is everywhere. She dies.

"It don't smell right," Elgin says. "Nothing spermy about it. Nothing eggy. It's not a person, it's an it."

ACT

THREE

XI

She dies. For the past three days and nights of storm I've sat in the belfry of The Sanctuary; the first day too weak to eat, the first night too fearful to sleep. Her death stands like a black kite dancing among shrieks. Around here whistles and bells are sometimes tied to kites. They make a racket above Puget Sound, or over bluffs where crash waves and gales.

Her death is real. No one will understand that; a few theater people, perhaps, a few storytellers. It is not the role that is murdered. *She* is murdered. And, since she was so much a part of me, and I a part of her, my own soul flees, then returns but timidly. There has not been much of *me* here these past three days; but gradually the self returns, cloaked in vestments of mourning.

Storm slams around the belfry, which is an unshuttered box eight by eight feet. The boss bell hangs central below a rack of tenors and a tinkler, and wind sets brass mouths atremble. There are almost enough bells for a bellringer to do something with. I remember a dark night once spent in Sitka during a wet Alaskan spring. There's a Russian Orthodox church in the center of that town. It has a full belfry.

At the time I was drunk, though not gravely so, and nerved beyond sleep. Booze electrified feelings. I wished not to be isolated on an island, talking to people who wanted radio ads in a town of six thousand.

The wind blew, and gusts sang handsome in the trees; Sitka spruce above brown bears, salmon in the seas. The bar across the street was staffed with hearty bawds, and fishermen and Indians.

I lay seeking sleep, regretting beer. Booze is unkind to the larynx. Actors and singers must show caution. Wind whooped and slammed. Indian spirits whispered. Also, Russian spirits, above forgotten echoes of muzzle-loading guns. The town is haunted.

And then the bells began. Midnight. Russian Easter. God had died, was now alive again. Alive.

A musical genius rang the bells, playing an instrument fine as his capacities. Bells can sing in the right hands, and song swept through the night. Song donned the robes of wind.

I rushed to the window. Bells surrounded me in clanks and tinkles and resonances of joy. The window looked onto the street, and for a moment ghostly resurrection walked the town. Dim light approached. Wind slammed. Faint voices sounded bold against the wind. I opened wide the window.

It was the congregation of the Russian church. They stepped singing along the street, and each person—even children—carried a candle. They held a hand cupped around each candle to avoid the wind.

It was blowing twelve to eighteen knots out there. I saw a miracle. There were surely two hundred candles. Not a one of them blew out. The congregation paraded steadily into the church. The final light disappeared behind closed doors, the bells fell silent. The world felt like a living thing. I slept.

This belfry of The Sanctuary stands dwarfed by modern business structures, but is tall enough a man can look across the storm-swept roof of Cathedral Mansion Hotel. The Soft Porn Grocery looks like flotsam cast on the flooded banks of the street. This belfry is host to constant winds, and may have once had shutters. If so, the winds won long ago.

Trouble and despair ring the neighborhood. Katie Van Loon ran away from home, got as far as Cathedral Mansion, was captured by her father. Jorge Ramirez still searches for Maria, but now he will not find her.

Van Loon, Katie's father, filed a complaint. Police hassled the owners of Cathedral Mansion. Police told the punks to mind their manners. Uneasy truce does not amount to much. It's all we have.

The Soft Porn Grocery was held up for a pittance. Police later figured it a diversion while someone raided offices at the truck axle company. The homosexual bar installed new neon. Now a pink figure, maybe female, leads a pink poodle across the face of the joint. Pink is not our favorite color.

For three days now I've stayed in the belfry, and huddled in an arctic sleeping bag. Storm pounds the steeple, strikes wind and rain in my face. Silk sends Hal with food. My friends know something awful happens, do not know what. They may believe Maria is still alive. They do not yet know the killer is unveiled. I've sat like a small Jehovah here on high, and watched Jericho.

The street is a metaphor of our troubles. I see that now. In our nation's past the Oregon Trail was the first great metaphor. Then the West was settled. Cars and pavement arrived. Our national metaphor became the road. Then our cities bundled together, the better to sell things to each other, and the street arrived with metaphoric virulence. We are on the downswing here in Jericho. As one critic mourned, "We have descended from the torment of Oedipus to the commonality of 'motherfucker.' "

For three days the murderer cruises the streets. The black van rises out of early darkness, stays on the street 'til midnight. The murderer takes dark pleasure from anonymity. The van will actually slow in order to catch a stoplight, sit in a lane beside a police car.

The van first appears as a dark blotch on a freeway ramp leading from the north end. When it appears, demonic voices reverberate through this belfry. It occurs to me I may be mad, the voices coming from my own mind. If that is true then I have a most creative mind. These voices turn the rain to steam. There are hosts of them, but three dominate as a hellish trinity. Like Ebenezer Scrooge, I hear spirits of the past, the present, and the future.

The voice of the past rumbles in Latin, Dutch, English, Indian, and Chinese. It is a mourning demon, moaning hapless over fallen dreams. Its voice is the strongest here. Sometimes it makes the bells tremble and resonate. This is a demon of sorrow. It may have once had eyes and a heart. It would level this city if it could. This is a demon of disappointment, a spirit that once carved wilderness. It shaped in the name of progress, of missionary dreams toward a righteous future.

The demon of the present is not basso but alto, a demon of torment. It has few words of its own, only catchphrases. It cries of commerce, and style, and melodrama. Its patter is mindless as signboards. When it wails too loudly its voice vibrates like wind among phone wires; and breaking, the wail flicks like snow on a TV screen; a disposable voice that gives no echo.

The demon of the future is soprano, a demon of fear. It was born without eyes or ears. While the demon of the present wails, this demon shrieks. I gather from its babble that there is no future.

The black van makes frequent stops. Young women climb in, ride for a while, and then climb out. Is the killer so selective that the proper girl and the proper moment must be found? The murderer could kill a half dozen girls each night. The girls seem to know the van, the driver; and gladness, or at least temporary thrill brings them to the van. Most of the women are selling, yet the van never stops long enough for them to deliver. What is so astounding is that they climb in without second thought. Usually a whore will pause long enough to check the john out. This murderer has been on the street for a long time, but so have we here at The Sanctuary. Surely we should know more about this than we do.

Two things are certain. I must organize my friends. I must also cast a role that will work in revealing evidence. The police have five hundred suspects. They will pay no attention to my accusations, even if I don the role of distinguished gentleman. They will pay no attention to me even if I take the role of retired detective. Besides, the police will foul up. They will make moves that will change the murderer's pattern before the pattern betrays enough evidence. Only hard evidence will serve.

After three days I've figured out *Who* my role will be. He is slightly liver-spotted, practical, a former high school teacher who loves the way pieces fit together. He is a World War II veteran, once a man of great importance. He is the world's leading authority on the nomenclature of World War II small arms. He knew which weapons were likely to fail, which ammunition was interchangeable. He could fieldstrip any Allied or enemy weapon in the dark. He was wounded in the thigh during the campaign in Italy, and he still walks with a limp. He was only a captain of infantry, but before the war concluded he was consulted by generals.

One thing more. It is time to descend into The Sanctuary and prepare the role, but I must say this. My heart is heavy with grief, and my thoughts ill. If I *were* a small Jehovah, would I stand in this belfry and hurl these demons into the storm-stricken street? Would I free their frenzies? Like Zeus flinging lightning bolts and thunder?

XII

We sit, the five of us, on the front steps of The Sanctuary as night lays dark paws on the street. My friends have been singing, and I'm accompanying them on trumpet. Tomorrow I will go into role.

Elgin appears in the dusk as a set of smiling white teeth, and the rest of my friends seem like small and faded clouds. A security light burns before the truck axle company. Vandermeer's estate nestles behind its chain-link fence. The Great Dane woofed all day, is presently woofless. It stands regarding the flow of headlights and taillights, listening to passing snatches of rock or country music from car radios. Jorge Ramirez starts his evening patrol, looking for Maria. Katie Van Loon is held captive in her room. That will not work, but we do not see Van Loon with many alternatives.

It is the time of vespers, of evensong. Hal will rise soon and perform his religious duties. Perhaps belov'ed Silk will join him. Hal is most fortunate of men. Silk acts as his mother.

"I feel bad for that amigo." Symptomatic Nerve Gas watches the diminishing figure of Jorge Ramirez. "If he was goin' to find Maria he would have."

There's nothing to say. How can I explain that the gods of theater sometimes grant me overreaching vision. I know where Maria lies. How do I explain? Besides, am I entitled to deny the Ramirez family its hope? The task now is to save Katie.

"A little clutch purse of stars up there," Elgin murmurs. He leans back looking at the sky. "Behold 'em quick, my friends, we've weather coming." He sniffs the air, then looks toward the homosexual bar and the pink poodle. "An affront to dogs," he whispers. "Dogs be mostly honest folk."

"We must become hounds." Hal's voice is low, and I do not catch his sense until I remember he is from Virginia. Doubtless Hal has ridden to the hounds. Doubtless Hal has quaffed a stirrup cup. Does Hal think of our killer as a fox?

"Not a chance," Silk says to Hal. "You have a more important job than dog-sniffing a murderer." She looks at Hal in the dim dark, and Hal is silent. "Suppose you find him," Silk says. "What will you do? Use that weapon? You are a defender, not an avenger."

We have never heard Silk speak so positively. Everyone here, including Hal—probably—understands that Silk protects Hal from himself. Silk is dead set against weapons, especially Hal's weapons. She is correct. If a murderer can kill forty girls with a knife, then a broadsword in skilled hands is no damned joke.

Elgin is first to pick up on the situation. He backs up Silk. "Sniffin' is honorable work," he says to Silk, and pretends his feelings are hurt. "Sniffin' is my game, woman." He turns to Hal. "Pay attention to the lady. We'll hunt the demon down. Do we need help we'll call."

"You can flush this crap about demons." Symptomatic Nerve Gas looks toward the homosexual bar where a flit in lavender tights displays his balls. The tights are built to shove his apparatus up and outward. Two other flits in pink and green party gowns pass him, nudge each other and giggle. "There's no such things as demons. We've got enough kinks to go around." Symptomatic Nerve Gas is dogmatic. He's almost obnoxious.

I finger my trumpet, place it to my lips, run a low question into the darkness. The trumpet is a good one. I've had it for years. Joshua had ram's horns when Jericho fell. I'd rather have the trumpet.

If only everything were as simple as Symptomatic Nerve Gas thinks. I remember the killer's hand on my shoulder, the violence, the machinelike clasp. Even now, days later, bruises have not disappeared and my shoulder aches. If the murderer is not a demon, it will serve until a real demon appears.

On the other hand, I'm probably crazy. I hear demons in the tower of The Sanctuary. This is the twentieth century, not the thirteenth. There's a certain amount of madness that enters into any kind of theater. At some time, in one role or another, I probably slipped into the gulf of insanity and never even noticed.

"You go sniffin' murderers, who protects the children?" Elgin talks to Hal, and Elgin is definitely in league with Silk. "Who protects the womens? You be no Tamburlaine, my man, nor neither the Lone Ranger." Elgin grins at me; a wide, doggy grin saying he has not forgotten the question of demons. He just doesn't want more talk about demons when Hal is around.

"That goes for you too." Symptomatic Nerve Gas speaks to Silk, and while his voice tries to be kind, the kindness is lost beneath rude urgency. "Don't you go sniffin' either. That sicko creep likes to kill women." Symptomatic Nerve Gas hears the crudity in his voice. "It's rougher than you think," he says helplessly. "It's complicated." Perhaps he remembers the corpses of Korean women, the devastation wrought by armies.

"It's vespers," Silk whispers to Hal. She stands, ready to enter The Sanctuary. She turns back to Symptomatic Nerve Gas as Hal stands to follow her. "Women protect their own." Her voice is soft. "You must allow me my woman's ways." She leaves us, and maybe prayer already forms on her lips. Hal follows.

My heart is more startled than my mind. Silk promises nothing. If she makes a mistake, and if something bad happens to Silk, then both of them are doomed. Hal believes himself an English gentleman. He was raised in Virginia. His codes are doubly fixed.

Hal could never strike a woman. He would cut his hand off if he did. He defends women. If so much as a hair of Silk's head is harmed, Hal will wreak revenge. I think of the song of that broadsword through the air. The steel in that thing is fine enough that Hal could dismember an elephant.

Symptomatic Nerve Gas has the same feelings. "Double shit," he says, "we'd better do something quick. Who would of thought she'd be contrary?"

"Me," Elgin tells him. "I had a black mammy." He stares skyward where the clutch of stars twinkle before an approaching cloud. "This is getting serious."

Elgin is tribal. In addition, Elgin is wise. This neighborhood would have more trouble than it does, were it not for Elgin. "We got two choices," he says. "Either we daddy-up to those two, and watch 'em every minute, or else we exorcise this demon." He looks toward Van Loon's house, which stands so dimly lit. "The daddy-style ain't working for Van Loon. Katie is just waiting to make a break. Why would daddying work for us?"

"Which means we've got one choice," I say.

"There's got to be a license plate on that van," Elgin says. "That's a place to start."

"Maybe they sell Holy Water at the Soft Porn." Symptomatic Nerve Gas is truly pissed. "You can sprinkle him. Poof." Talk of demons is an insult to our man.

"Think of it this way." Elgin talks directly at the moon. "Old moon has seen a thousand million die, and tons of them abruptly. War and murder. Moon's seen inquisitions." He looks at Symptomatic Nerve Gas. "You've known the same as moon, seen things not human."

Anger stilled, Symptomatic Nerve Gas sits. No doubt he recalls the retreat from P'yŏngyang, ten thousand gallons of blood on snow.

"We got demons, brother, 'cause we make 'em." Elgin reaches to touch hands with Symptomatic Nerve Gas. "Demons are the spirits of their times."

I have not thought of this. Maybe I'm not crazy after all. Maybe every century builds its own heavens and hells, or maybe only hells. Maybe each generation constructs its own demons.

"Olden days saw gargoyles on the church. They miseried the demons." Elgin points to the steeple of The Sanctuary. "These days we don't need gargoyles there. Our demons cruise the bricks."

Symptomatic Nerve Gas is silent, but I can see grudging acceptance on his face. The man can handle abstractions. It's just that his tongue won't wrap around them. "Okay," he says, "call it a demon. The point is, what the hell do we do about it?"

"I'll be about some sniffin'," Elgin says. "I'll talk to folks."

"It'll scent the hounds," I say. "You talk to folks, it's bound to hear."

Elgin watches the stars. One by one they are picked off by scudding clouds. "I'm no spring chicken, nor layer, either. I can take chances." He turns to Symptomatic Nerve Gas. "Can you ruin a van without dilapidating anyone inside?"

Symptomatic Nerve Gas grins.

"We may want to slow that—whatever it is."

"I can slow the sonovabitch into reverse."

"Don't do it yet," Elgin says. "Just be *ready* to do it. Get some tools together."

"I'm about to go into role," I tell them. "It's a role that ought to help."

Elgin is respectful, but he still has something to say. "There's a moment comes when hunted ones turn into hunters. Happens when the hunted has nothing more to lose, or maybe too much. You ready to hunt?"

"I'll be walking with a slight limp," I tell them, "and I'll be a man who likes the way things fit. I'll put the book together on our demon. Don't worry about the limp. It's just a part of the role."

XIII

My limp does not gimp, it swings. I'm the King of Swing; and the first law of the street is to keep moving. If you stop you become a target. You interrupt the regular flow. It's been that way since young Athens, probably, certainly since Rome. The flow comes from a mixture of time-senses. Each person out here has a mission, and cadences rise from all those missions. Indian winos search for pet frogs they lost when they first hit town, or walk thinking of tides. Kids are on the run even when standing around rapping. On the street there's no place to rest. If you have money and a bath, you can sit in a restaurant. Otherwise, keep moving.

I have money and a bath. The past three days have been too busy to take advantage of either. There may be rest for the wicked, there is none for the researcher. It's pleasing to see how much you can get done if you work steadily, and if you know how to steer bureaucrats. Bureaucrats are good-hearted people, mostly, and many of them know they engage in bullshit. One need only look respectable, speak with authority, and show a bit of moxie.

It was easy research, but time-consuming. I walked the street at night, waiting for the van to pass. The next day I traced the license on the van. I picked up the name and address of the owner at vehicle registration. Then I checked tax records on the house. After that, things got interesting. I found leads to a sleazy real estate agency. That caused me to do a lot more checking. Our murderer may be two murderers; man and wife, or brother and sister. A lot of property is owned by two people with unremarkable last names, but their first names are Joe and Josie.

This is a snazzy role, and I'm having fun. My gentleman is less "proper" than I thought likely. He's more of a realist, but with streaks of romance and a slight stench of the gutter. It's a fascinating combination. His jacket is English tweed, his slacks tailored wool. He affects an English motoring cap which he does not need, and carries an ornate walking stick which he does need. At times his limp is barely discernible, but in the last twenty-four hours another storm front moves in. The limp increases. Old folks used to call the condition lumbago. It's really rheumatism.

I am fascinated by his mind, which may have been wasted in a lifetime of teaching high school. After all, how much can you teach? Discourse with teenagers has never been my idea of prime time. The kids are so glandular, so filled with liquids. We once nominally controlled the males by telling them masturbation would make them go blind, or make hair grow on their palms. Society runs on lies. In other days our lies were functional.

However, this is no time to worry about whether the man has wasted his life. It is time to enjoy the role.

Even murderers have to eat. When murderers drive expensive vans they have to buy or steal them. Our murderer makes her living, or his living, or *its* living in a manner fit for a contemporary demon. It's a sleaze merchant.

Foreclosures are not new in history. This particular joker frequents sheriff's sales. Tricky bumfuzzling goes on. Sophisticated sleaze. There's nothing new in taking real estate at bargain prices, having winos put on a hundred bucks' worth of bad paint, dropping three hundred with a plumber; then turning the mess over to a real estate agency. Our murderer does this routinely. The sophisticated part is what's interesting. I almost admire the sad little sack.

In every city small parcels of land fall between surveys, or are rendered useless by other construction. Corporations build offices, then landscape areas, and forget the fifteen square feet unaccounted for in any survey. Or, the state will run a road. Where the road connects with another road, a little triangle of land may not properly fall within the right-of-way. These patches and pockets of land lie unused for so many years they become technically unowned. Or, they may be owned, but deemed completely useless. No reason to pay taxes. Our murderer picks them up for prices from ten to a thousand dollars. It requires research to find them, but our murderer's days are free.

Once you have the land you pull a heist. Fifteen square feet of a corporation's park or plaza can fetch a thousand dollars a square foot. If the corporation doesn't believe it, you erect a cheesy tent on your fifteen square feet and camp out. You gypsy-up the landscape. Or a triangle of land at an intersection can hold a skinny billboard, or a shanty, or piles of driftwood on the pretext of constructing modern art. You force the state to buy its own mistake. Real estate for fun and profit. The American Way.

The American Way used to be different. I wait at a bus stop, destination the north end. I want to walk past our murderer's house. I want focus, like the narrowing view through a Schmidt and Bender rifle scope. I want to center in on our girlfriend, or boyfriend; because we are going to highball this cookie into the enjoyment of a lethal injection. We are going to take this fuckface out.

I may be an old man, but it's nice to be thinking like a young one; thinking young, yet serene in my seventy-some years' worth of guile. At my back rises a boarded-up building slated for destruction. Bullet marks pock the concrete walls. Street people hang around. Jerks deal drugs. This was the site of a drive-by shooting. One drug-dealing kid was killed.

All you have to do is look at the bullet marks on the side of this building, and you see what's gone wrong with our world. The traces go straight across, make a line maybe thirty feet long. The fire was distributed across a wide field. Very ineffective.

The first modern machine guns date to 1900. Russians and Japs used them in '04–'05. The biggest advances in small-arms technology came between 1890 and 1910. Everything since is variations on a theme.

The machine gun puts down a cone of fire. That's the philosophy. Some models of the Jap Nambu didn't even traverse. The machine gun concentrates on strong points; the mouth of a ravine, village streets, roads and road junctions, paths in a forest, the face of a pillbox. Those beasties of 1904 could lay two hundred to three hundred rounds per minute into an area the size of your front door. It was called "fire superiority." Like a long-range shotgun.

You've got no fire superiority if your fire distributes away from your target, the way the marks are distributed on this wall. A single rifleman can beat you. Misuse of the machine gun is a symbol of disintegration. We're shooting the shit out of everything, but it's random fire.

I board the bus and take a seat at the rear. Up front are seats reserved for old folks and cripples. You have to be pretty old, or pretty crippled, or pretty goddamn dumb to sit in them. When somebody decides to beat on the bus driver the hassle ends in your brittle lap. It's a fad, these days, beating on bus drivers.

As the bus pulls from the stop Elgin stands before a thrift shop. He's been talking to people for three days. Now he talks to a drunk. The drunk wears two topcoats and the remains of a red felt hat. Elgin plays casual, maybe even funny. The drunk looks pretty drunk. Elgin will get some kind of information.

This bus is a moving-picture show. There's the show beyond the windows, and the show inside. We've got a bloody travelogue going on out there; shades of Richard Haliburton, Martin and Osa Johnson, Amundsen, Lindbergh, Perry. I think of them because their explorations came together in the 1920s. I think of the 1920s because these early Nineties are like the Eighties, and the Eighties were carbon copies of the Twenties. People think they've invented something. They're only replaying history.

The Twenties saw adventure and illicit booze. In the Eighties we saw space flight and illicit drugs. In the Twenties two economies ran: the regular economy and the cash economy of the alkie cookers. Same thing today. Hundreds of millions in drug cash running unaccounted, pointing to an economic bust. The Twenties and Eighties saw gang wars, and breakdown of families. The Twenties saw the advent of ballyhoo. Today we call it hype.

The bus passes skin stores, Viet restaurants, joints teaching karate and kung fu. Plywood fences surround construction, the fences littered with playbills, movie posters, gang graffiti; plus some original stuff: "Y'all repent now, ya hear?" The bus moves to a classier section, boutiques, stores selling cameras, ritzy places peddling future antiques: Lladró, Baleek, Royal Copenhagen, and Japanese Noritake. I don't like Japs very much, and I sure don't like Krauts. Why any Jew would buy a Mercedes-Benz or a Volkswagen is more than this child can figure.

The classier section does not last. The street changes to walkup apartments and crack houses. Sanitizing signs infest light poles. Signs explain fines for littering, jaywalking, failure to clean up dog poop. Signs seem desperate to regulate all behavior: no loitering, no skateboards, no booze in public. Two blocks away The Sanctuary raises its steeple above a world so filled with corruption, it's become preoccupied with being puerile. We are overrun with sanitizers.

The show going on inside this bus is a wee example. Signs read "no smoking," "no beverages," "no pets," "no ice cream," "no loud talk," "no radios." Posters warn of heart disease, cancer, emphysema, rape, child abuse, AIDS, anorexia. Society has become tighter than a bull's ass in fly time.

Shades of Carrie Nation. The feminist movement is what causes this mind-laundering. Give the girls a little power and they act as badly as men. The whole society is henpecked. It's a long ride to the north end but the bus finally makes it. Before leaving the main drag I stop in a church foyer and pick up pamphlets. It's always best to have a cover story. If anyone questions me, I'll spin a yarn about being a retired missionary.

I walk through a residential neighborhood looking for our murderer's address. Houses here are nice enough. Tricycles park on barbered lawns. Camper trucks, motorboats on trailers; a few TV satellites roof-perching like enormous catcher's gloves. You get occasional glimpses of little kids staring from windows, or young mothers sitting in kitchens. They drink coffee and try to remain sane. There's a chill in the air. It's beginning to drizzle.

If I were a murderer this is the sort of neighborhood I'd choose for a hideout. The biggest things happening around here are garden hoses that bust, or wars waged against dandelions.

Our murderer isn't trying to hide. I swing my limp to a slow foxtrot, cruising the sidewalk on the other side of the street. The murderer's house shimmers in Day-Glo green with rose trim. It's split-level, hiding behind a four-foot laurel hedge and among young firs. There's a two-car garage with the doors open. The black van stands in the garage displaying its zitty demons. The thing doesn't look like much in daylight. Our murderer owns two vehicles, because the empty parking space in the garage is uncluttered.

I rest on my walking stick, pretending age and fatigue. It's not a hard act to play. That joint is strictly tinkerbell, worse than a Chrysler Airflow with whitewalls: plastic duckies parade across the lawn. The mailbox is a deep basket with decorated wooden lid, Honduran fakey. Windows are thermopane boxed in aluminum frames, and surrounded by plastic trim. A plastic birdbath stands beneath a plastic birdhouse. The bath is shaped like a cornucopia, the birdhouse imitates a Victorian hotel. Very cutesy. Some asshole cut the top out of a seventy-foot fir and mounted a TV antenna. The tree actually looks embarrassed.

I take a deep breath and nearly slip out of role. I've sold an awful lot of trash in my life. How many times has the murderer seen me pitch something on TV, then rushed right out and bought it? If not an accessory to murder, I'm certainly an accessory to bad taste.

I potter along the sidewalk and figure the next move. It's necessary to see the inside of that house. Are the walls filled with framed photos of all the murdered girls? There's bound to be something incriminating in there.

The advantage is all mine, because of guile. Nobody recognizes guile these days. Everything's too obvious, and you can take the Uzi hand weapon as an example. It's a blowback piece of disposable junk firing from a closed bolt. Its name sounds like a Greek hangover, but it's imported from Israel; from those gentle folk who once brought you Sodom and Gomorrah. The Uzi carries no guile, and frickin' little function. It's like the 1937 French Chauchat. Use it 'til you get a blockage, then throw the bugger away.

If you want guile, consider the American model 1 derringer. That's me. I'm a derringer.

In a way this is fun. The actor is in role, and now the role takes on a role. I'm going to play a missionary bringing glad tidings of the Lord to the middle-middle class here in rain-town. This is a play within a play within a play.

Drizzle continues. The scheme is to start at the corner of the block, knock on doors, pass out tracts and speak of the Second Coming. The murderer will not suspect anything from an old missionary putzing around the neighborhood. It's a groove. It's a gas. It's snazzy. It's the bee's knees.

In addition, it goes well. The first house contains a timid little housewife dreaming dreams. She has two kids, and she's pregnant. TV broadcasts soap: "Oh, Edward, do you really think we *must.*" An actress edges toward a bedroom. The housewife dreams. Actors have no morals. They will take any kind of work. Edward looks like a highly polished turd wearing a thousand-dollar rug. The housewife keeps track of the tube as I murmur about Sunday school. Her two kids holler and blow snot.

Someone is home in the second house, but no one answers the doorbell. Lots of people hole up these days.

The third is home to a woman of fifty, plus a covey of cats and a pit bull that eyes me like I'm delicious. An antique 45-70 Springfield holds the spot of honor above a fireplace. A gun cabinet displays an Allen Henry 44-40, a Bushmaster .223 auto, and a Heckler & Koch HK-91. Some numbnut is ready for the next war. The woman carries that beat-down look people get when they've lived too long beside freaks. I say a few words in behalf of salvation, doubt anything will come of them.

The fourth house holds a young jock in lavender running togs. He's probably riding unemployment and his wife's paycheck. He looks at me, shakes his head, closes the door in my face in a way that says he can't believe what he's just seen. We're in agreement.

One more to go. The fifth house sits right next door to the murderer's house. This is a cottage, windowboxes neatly cleaned. Next spring will see daffodils and tulips. I feel bulbs snore beneath neatly swept soil. An ancient hemp mat lies before the door. You could smoke it and get high. Paint is clean, the doorknob polished.

She's tiny and old, with blue eyes clear as wind across prairie, and she reports herself as a Baha'i from Montana. We hold curious conversations as I begin a Methodist rap about our Lord. "Sit down," she says. "If you're a missionary, I'm Greta Garbo." She wears a housedress, and it's classy. It's the kind of housedress you have to iron, ruffles and all. Our grandmothers used to wear such dresses, skirts to the floor. This dress is light blue like her eyes, and her tiny feet are encased in soft slippers; real leather, not black naugahyde. This may be the last true lady left alive. She dresses correctly, even when she's only staying home.

"A real missionary doesn't start by giving tracts," she tells me. "He would carry the Good Book. He'd have a little cross pinned to his lapel, and would not carry a walking stick with an ivory head. I expect you're running a con." She motions to a needlepoint chair, and I sit obedient as a kid in a dunce cap. "We're old enough that we don't need so many rules," she says. "Coffee, tea, or a beer?"

"It's pretty early in the day," I say. A beer? From a Baha'i? When we're being religious?

"At our age," she tells me, "it's always early. We're right at the beginning of something new." She moves slowly to the kitchen, and I sit completely stopped. Sure as anything, she's going to turn me into an alcoholic Baha'i.

"I'm a private detective," I tell her, and wonder if she hears. Rustles in the kitchen, faucet running, the tinkle of saucers and cups. This living room is enough to bring tears from an old man. A china cabinet holds stuff that should be in a museum. Furniture is Victorian but not massive. You don't have to starch good lace, and the lace here lies comfortably and glowing across arms of chairs. An old-timey sampler ornaments the wall, and a couple of alcohol lamps flash polished brass. A worn oriental rug presses color into the room. Leather-bound books, and a few library books, cluster in a sidearm desk. There's Indian trinkets, and, so help me, a stereopticon with slides. The only thing out of place is a perfectly weighted Navajo loom. Somebody helped her with those weights. Work stretches on the loom, a rug no bigger than a welcome mat.

She returns with a silver tea service. It's so heavy her hands shake, but she gets it in place on a low table. ("Don't die.") I say it in my mind where she can't hear. ("You are the very last survivor of something that was once so precious.") I actually don't say anything. Thinking to myself.

She's old. She's from another time. She's a passenger pigeon. I'm a passenger pigeon. We're on our way to becoming extinct.

Screw this wacky, snafu world. It doesn't deserve us, won't miss us, and there's comfort in that. The greatest victory is to withdraw. Leave the kiddies to play in their own mud puddles.

Still, there's a job to do. She has a murderer living next door. She must know something. If she's from Montana, and has still managed to live this long, she can't help but be wise. I think of Montana, of buttes and streams and deer, of shit-kicking music, booze, and pickup trucks, poetry and rednecks. Billings has become an overgrown Woolworth's. Missoula displays drunken poets; the iambics of heaven, laced with shotglasses of hell.

She pours tea. Her hands tremble only a little. They are such small hands. I sit and remember Teeney. Teeney is dead. Teeney was about the size of this lady. If Teeney had lived, might she have grown old and expressed such grace? I'm getting all mixed up. The actor is inside the role. The role remembers high school kids. Year after year of high school kids, how precious they are; how excited and zitty and awkward and filled with plans. They are so beautiful; and you try to give them a little sense of history, a little sense of who they are, where they come from. Otherwise they have no history. Except the street.

"Honesty is not only the best policy," she tells me, "it's the only policy I'll speak to. You may be trying to detect something, but you're no detective." She offers me tea, glances toward the Navajo loom. "My first husband was an Indian."

She's telling me to be direct. Indians are direct. Even when they bullshit.

"Someone is killing young women," I tell her. "I think he—or maybe she—lives next door. The green and pink house. I don't mean to frighten you."

Now she is genuinely sad, certainly not scared. "Lies frighten me. I'm too old to be afraid of anything else."

This is not the way things are supposed to go. I find myself telling her most of the story. Teeney, Maria, our fears for Katie. I've got the historian's sense of matters. The way I condense and pull it together is just wonderful. By the end of a second cup of tea she has almost all of it.

"He's an actor," she says quietly when I finish. "Only one person lives there. When he mows his yard he's a man. When he goes to the grocery he's a woman. People wish he would move, but he's been here so long we don't much pay attention." She is momentarily apologetic. "I was never one to butt into people's business."

You can bet she wasn't. You can bet she has always tended her own fences. That used to be part of the American ethic, although it was never pure. She momentarily seems even older and more frail. Then discipline takes over. Her hands rest folded in her lap. Her wrinkled mouth is firm. "I thought he was nothing but a scamp. I've known other people who were *really* crazy."

I haven't mentioned demons, and I haven't told the true number of murders. I'm admitting to nothing right now. She would think *I'm* crazy.

"I'll tell what I know. I'll not gossip." Her face carries such sadness. She is not accusing me. I'm accusing myself. This woman has got to be eighty, and I've laid this fresh bunch of trouble in her lap. She has earned the right not to have to listen to this.

"He buys things," she tells me. "I've never known a body to buy so many things."

That figures. We've got the ultimate consumer on our hands. If plastic duckies in the yard don't prove it, the plastic birdhouse does. Five will get you ten our Good-Time Charlie even has plastic birds. No self-respecting wren would even crash in that thing. "Buys things?" I ask. "What kinds of things?"

"Deliveries from department stores two and three times a week. Antique stores bring furniture. He brings home outlandish garden tools. Packages in the mail. Jennie, across the street, sells Avon. She's run out of new things to sell him."

Jennie, who lives across the street. She will have been inside the house, in case I don't get inside. I shouldn't be acting the role of missionary. I should be a Fuller Brush man. This guy is strictly not hep.

I'm overstaying my welcome, but this woman is too fine a lady to mention it. Her frail hands tremble. She is fatigued. When age rolls over you, the body no longer does what the mind wants. You tend to take naps, to pace yourself. I've visited her while spewing this crap, and completely spoiled her morning. She's tired. Even catching the murderer does not warrant placing more burden on her.

"There's a little story I enjoy," she says. She gives it like a gift. A present to a departing guest. What do I have that I could possibly give?

"It's about two Chinese monks," she tells me. "There used to be a lot of Chinese in Montana. The story probably came from them." Her wrinkled face is alive, like she's telling a joke. "One monk meditated for twenty years learning to walk on water. This puzzled the other monk. He could not figure why the first one spent twenty years learning something so simple. For a few pennies he could be carried across the river on a ferry."

So much for the missionary business. It's kaput. I feel the strength of what she tells me, and haven't the foggiest notion what it means. One thing it means is I've something more to think about.

As I thank her I feel about as graceful as a fifteen-year-old. It's a flaming wonder I don't trip, or knock over china, or bump into furniture.

"You should stay away from his house," she tells me. "He's acting peculiar the past two days."

That pussycat is peculiar, okay. If he's different the past two days, then he's stacking peculiar on top of peculiar.

"He's almost frenzied," she tells me. "He drives away in his car, and then comes screeching back home. Then he becomes *her* and screeches away. It's awfully erratic. Always before, he's stayed home mornings."

"One last question. Does he bring people home with him? Does he bring women home?"

"He's completely solitary," she tells me. "I don't think he has a single friend. Nobody ever goes there."

XIV

Drizzle becomes light rain, but who's to care. I wear good wool. The problem isn't rain, it's Elgin. I stand before the murderer's house as worry spreads across my world. If the murderer acts peculiar there's a reason. That reason can only come because the murderer smells pursuit. First, an upper-middle-class white lady followed the murderer to the public market. Now Elgin asks questions. The street has its own message centers. Word has gotten back to our demon. Our demon is probably only confused at present, but will soon get dangerous. It could pick Elgin off with no more thought or trouble than it gives to picking its nose.

Still, it's a shame to waste a long bus ride. The house sits surrounded by plastic, and it's clear no one's home. It's also clear the murderer could come screeching in at any minute. Christopher Columbus took a chance, so why shouldn't I?

On the other hand, Columbus' chance paid off. If our demon feels pursued, it isn't going to buy any stories about missionaries. I picture myself in an enormous iron pot surrounded by demons, my goose slowly being cooked..

It's so easy to ask for trouble. I waltz my limp up the walkway to the house while thinking Bible-thoughts. Some biblical historians insist Jericho was in ruins two hundred years before Joshua arrived. They insist the Good Book runs a scam; takes credit for the destruction in order to demonstrate Jehovic power. They could be right, but what difference? Jericho was buggered either way.

The front porch gives double reason to rejoice. Drapes fall aside so the living room is easily seen. The mailman has made delivery. The tacky mail basket sits stuffed with catalogs, flyers, magazines—*Glamour, Cosmo, Cavalier, Sports Illustrated, Guns and Ammo;* and, praise be, a bank statement that slides easily into the inner pocket of my jacket. You can learn a lot from a bank statement.

The living room is early Sears. Ethan Allen. I mentally paraphrase a leading expert. "Sears has done for bullshit what Stonehenge did for rocks." There's a television half the size of the wall. On top of it, and mixed in with tacky maple furniture, and cutesy patterned fabric, are photos of our murderer. This cat is in love with himself—itself. Photos show it as a high-class female singer before a jazz combo. They show it in boxing trunks and robe, standing in a ring while a phony referee raises its right hand. The murderer is pictured skiing, is seen in a Formula 1 race car, is seen in long gown and with sexy smile, hanging on the arm of a state senator, is seen on horseback with its nose sticking from beneath a cowboy hat, is seen as both male and female models; and seen posturing as a cop, a sax player, a karate black belt, and a street whore. There's some comfort for me in the photographs. Each one is insincere. This lollipop is not, strictly speaking, an actor. These are not roles, they're fantasies.

I wiggle the doorknob, am relieved to find it locked. If it were open I'd be just stupid enough to step inside. Momma never raised me to be a detective, anyway. Drapes on the other side of the doorway are closed, but there's a little open space at the corner of the window. If you lean forward it's possible to see a narrow view in the unlighted bedroom.

The bed is made. An imitation patchwork quilt, in colored prints with machine stitching, lies like an ad for condoms. A genuine antique highboy in cherry wood sits beside a lady's makeup table, art noveau, circa 1920s. Neatly arranged on the table, beside jars of makeup and perfume, lie three knives. One is a stiletto, one a brass-bound folding woods knife, and the third is a short-bladed combat knife. Rangers use those things. So do secret agents and mercenaries and survivalists. A five-inch blade doesn't sound like much, but the blade is double-edged and two inches wide. You could gut a steer.

Time to get out. Those are carefully chosen knives. Each asks its own technique. Our murderer may not know jack-shit about anything else, but you can bet he knows knives.

I potter along to the front sidewalk, thinking of knives, making my getaway. Krauts always hated cold steel. By the time World War II came around, the bayonet was obsolete. The only reason we carried the things is because they scared the Teutonic shit out of Krauts. There's something in the German mind that goes terror stricken before a blade. At the same time, those dumb brew meisters will stand up to machine guns.

The front sidewalk lies like a path away from trouble. Rain tick, tick, ticks, and it's time to head for cover. The laurel hedge glistens with honest green, the house glowers with dishonest green. A garbage can sits stuffed beside the garage. Parts of broken things, plastic and wood and glass, consumed, discarded. It would be possible to step inside that garage, and, if caught, claim to be hiding from the weather.

I'm about to make a dumb decision, but a smart one is made for me. Two blocks away an XK-140 Jag corners hard enough for the rear end to break. It's a beautiful car, built back in the days when the English still showed some class. It is a collector's item, but right now it's being driven with no more thought than you'd give to a Nipponese racing scow with soft valve seats. It's painted English racing green. The guy jumps hard on second gear and tires smoke on wet pavement. That Jag is not a flat-course car. It has no place in the city. It's a road car that should be training for the Mille Miglia.

In the Thirties, the glory days of racing, the Italian racing color was red. American cars didn't play in those days, but later our racing colors became blue. Now our young turks use anything, even orange. The Krauts' racing color used to be white, and back in the Thirties they won every race they entered. Hitler developed the engine for Stuka dive-bombers on the racetracks of Europe. Peacetime research for military purposes. Nothing ever changes.

The Jag pops against its gears, slows, hangs a left into the garage. Exhaust mutters on a fast idle, the delightful puttering of a well tuned engine. Krauts used to call that sound *Auspuff*. The engine dies, our murderer steps out. I lean on my walking stick and pull my hat down, as if minding my own business while avoiding rain.

It's the same murderer who destroyed my lady in the public market. If I had a pistol I'd end this right now while thinking revenge, and spend the rest of my life repenting. It's one thing to take a guy out because he's got it coming, quite another to take him out in a fury of hatred.

There is no doubt about his identity, although this time he's a man. Even if there were doubt, he couldn't conceal that nose, which is the important feature of his face. He reaches into the car, pulls out a hatbox. It probably holds a wig. He's probably getting his act together for Mardi Gras. Every phony in town crawls from his crack on Fat Tuesday. Next time we see this guy he'll be a redhead, or a black-haired Spanish maid. Right now he's a muscular but skinny dude dressed in designer jeans and sport jacket. The jeans have pink stitching around the crotch, and his shoes are black loafers—with tassels for God's sake—and I've known Dobermans who looked kindlier.

He stands watching me like he thinks of committing murder in this midday drizzle. He won't, but he doesn't try to hide the desire. I've never seen such contempt on a face. If he's smart enough to evade the police for years, he's smart enough to do his killing else-where. Still, I'm a stranger to this neighborhood. He's memorizing the way I look. When he comes hunting for Elgin, he'll also come hunting for me. This bum is about to destroy another one of my roles, and precious little I can do about it. I potter away, limping like the close of a dance marathon. It doesn't pay to look back. It pays to get over to the main drag and hail a bus.

I board the bus conscious that I'm half in role and half out of role. It's a nowhere state for actors, a sort of purgatory between identi-ties. Lots of actors have no real self. If they had an essential self they wouldn't be actors. That's never been a problem for me. My problem has always been that I have too many selves. Right now, one of those selves analyzes the situation.

We're fools to take this killer on. As the bus heads for down-town, fear and worry become about equal. This guy can kill Elgin, Silk, Symptomatic Nerve Gas; and he can mop me up like a dollop of spilled nose drops. He's young, we're not so young; and we've got to keep Hal out of it. Nobody will protect us. Nobody even knows we exist. We're street people.

If the first rule of the street is to keep moving, the second rule is to stay with the crowd. You don't have to speak to people, you don't have to like them, but you have to stay where they congre-gate. Become isolated and you're a target. You can be killed for the dime in your pocket, or killed just on the chance you might have a dime. You can be killed because somebody is powered up on crack, or because some kid shows off for other kids. The street is never safe, but you can live on it if you play by the rules.

Now we break one of the rules. The third rule of the street is to stay out of other people's business. I've walked past a thou-sand drug deals and never raised my eyes. I've seen men beat their women, and women stab their men. I've seen cops tear winos apart with nightsticks, just wrecking guys for the sheer pleasure of copping around. Survival out here means anonymity and blinders.

The murderer's bank statement rests in my jacket pocket. When I regain the role I'll check the bank statement. The actor is no good at analyzing this, but my old gentleman will be very good indeed. My gentleman is a tough old nut, a lot tougher than the actor. He's canny, he's filled with guile.

Meanwhile, the chase begins; but, oh Lord, the wrong man gets chased. From the back windows of the bus it is easy to see a green XK-140 hovering back there in traffic. The murderer goes nowhere fast. He tails the bus waiting for an old man to descend. When that old gentleman hits the bricks the murderer has options. He can kill in broad daylight, or he can follow his victim home. One thing is certain, my old gentleman can go nowhere near The Sanctuary. He cannot lead that monster to Elgin and Silk and Symptomatic Nerve Gas.

The actor fumbles for options. He can shed some clothing, do a transfiguration. The actor can get rid of hat, jacket, walking stick. He can make up as a bum, or a purse snatcher. He can walk briskly, descend from the bus with a jump, hop, and skip. The actor can do a lot more than that. Our murderer will be easy to fool.

On the other hand, the role is important. It is not simply a matter of theater, it's practical. My old gentleman can figure moves the actor cannot. My old gentleman is not finished with his work.

On still another hand, the murderer may get smart. Suppose he drives ahead of the bus, gets from the Jag, then boards the bus. My old gentleman would have no chance. I have to think; and what I think has to be quick and it has to be right.

What do we know about this guy? We know he's a murderer. We know he's a consumer. We know he is awash in fantasy. He drives a classic racing car. We know he's suspicious, but he does not know who is after him, or why. Lots of games and guises run around the street. All of his information says older people chase him. He's not nearly as afraid as he is indignant. After all, how can he give much credit to a Yankee dowager, an aging black man, and an old putz on a walking stick?

The actor relaxes. The murderer is not going to get from his car. It's ten-to-one he's hovering in traffic fantasizing that he's James Bond. That fancy Jag is perfect for the illusion. If he's a consumer he sits behind that wheel thinking the way he dresses puts him in deep cover. He's probably pretending he's an internationally famous tennis player who works as a spy. He thinks about which weapons he should carry, which disguises he should don. The fancy car is the key to the fantasy. He isn't going to leave that car.

It's time to get back into role. Not an easy job. You have to concentrate, really focus. I lean back in the seat, close my eyes, reach for my old gentleman, and allow him to gather me in.

World War II was a white man's war. So was Korea. The myth running in those days said Negroes wouldn't fight. Viet Nam was a black man's war. An awful lot of grunts got greased proving to Whitey they could fight.

I look back on WW II with sadness. Military doctrine will tell you that an outfit taking 35 percent casualties ceases to function as a fighting unit. In WW II our guys sometimes took 80 percent casualties and still kept moving on the enemy. The difference, back then, was that we still had something worth fighting for.

I look into the street. Our families have ceased to exist. Dogmeat guys in BMWs cruise, and talk about saving the world by selling it. Punks with Encom Mp-45 autos tear around like John Wayne with a rupture. Bureaucrats leave nothing untouched, and none of them know enough to fieldstrip a rubber from their own wangers. It ain't worth fighting for.

Plus, war has changed. These days it's all statistics. That was inevitable given smokeless powder, boat-tailed bullets, and soft extraction. Rimless ammo works best in light automatics, and I've seen some rare duckies in my time: the St. Etienne, the White, the Johnson, the Finnish Suomi. Lots of miracle ways to dust populations.

* * *

As the role deepens the mind moves above the bus and along the street. The street runs everywhere, and the big secret about the street is that the word is never plural. It's all one street.

The street twists, intersects, turns; pounded by tires and pounded by feet. Rain glosses the street from gray to black, and rain washes at spit gobs, cigarette butts, gum wrappers, religious tracts—the effluvia of gutters. In this gray city umbrellas come in fancy colors, so the street looks like acres of dancing tulips. Crowds thin as people cram into stores, restaurants, bars, to wait out the rain. Wind rises. The street is packed with wind. Blow, wind, blow and crack your cheeks. Sweep at filthy air, sweep smoke from the skies. Dance a whirlwind. Our troubled lives lie sprawled.

Van Loon, Katie's father, leans on the counter of a pawnshop. Before him lie a .38 police special, a Colt .45 auto, and a 9mm Beretta auto. Van Loon has thick hands to match his wide Dutch frame. His blue eyes hold the skill of a man accustomed to bargaining, but they hold sadness and fear as well. He touches the pistols as one might touch forbidden things. The pawnshop owner has made his pitch. He's smart enough not to oversell. Outside the pawnshop a cop writes a ticket for dog doo. A resigned citizen stands, leash in hand, muttering, "Down, Brutus," to a Yorkshire terrier. The .38 nestles like a toy in Van Loon's thick hand. The hand is still weak, but healing. It was fractured on a biker's forehead. Van Loon hesitates. The pawnshop owner throws in a box of cartridges. The deal is made.

Deeper into the street Elgin sits in an apartment doorway talking to an ancient black lady. A young woman and her pimp push past them, then climb stairs. Elgin and the old woman speak of days when they were young. The lady's hair is cotton-color, her housedress blue. "It's a good thing to be old and headed for Jesus," she says. "A body won't have to put up with all this here." Elgin watches the street. "There's lots of this-and-that these days. I feature what you mean."

Katie Van Loon slips through the back doorway of her house. She carries one change of clothes wrapped in a towel. Her blue eyes in her round face reflect fatigue. She should not be so tired, yet be so young. She knows that no one understands her, does not know she does not understand herself. She crosses the backyard and disappears down an alley, headed away from Cathedral Mansion Hotel. Katie walks rapidly toward the street.

On the street young girls are known as meat, slits, holes. They are traded for drugs, are sold as punching bags. Life expectancy for a young girl on the street is six months maximum, usually a lot less. Katie does not know this, and would not believe it if she did.

Behind The Sanctuary, Symptomatic Nerve Gas bends over the engine of a '67 Buick station wagon as rain patters on the hood. The car is a ragged-out wreck purchased for fifty dollars; but it weighs two tons and has enough remaining moxie to hit speeds of forty. Loaded in the station wagon are phosphorus, pure nitrogen fertilizer, motor oil, dynamite caps, a couple of ice picks, a handle for a bumper jack, a logging chain, and other items. Symptomatic Nerve Gas feels rain drip from the raised hood onto the back of his Army shirt. He mutters to himself. He prepares to stop a black van, and he has a number of imagined situations in mind. He tries to anticipate every likely scenario.

Three blocks away a cop writes a ticket for an unlicensed bicycle. A drug deal passes at his back. The two kids look his way, flip the bird, while passersby cast gazes to the sidewalk like they are intent on looking for dropped pennies.

Silk sits across from a young woman as they sip coffee in a fast-food restaurant. A TV monitor flickers above their heads. Today Silk dresses down as she attempts to mix with the street. She wears jeans and a bulky sweater, but her eyes reveal too much kindness and hurt. They are the eyes of a mother who has suddenly realized her own ignorance, and who does not know what to do. Silk thinks of The Sanctuary. "I've been in your place," she says to the young woman, and her lie has generous intent. "It pays to get out."

The young woman chews on a burger, but not hungrily. She chews as if she's forgotten how to eat. Her hair is black and Italian-curly. Beneath makeup her face is pale, and her lips are thin as blades when she chews. "It's a living," she tells Silk. "What am I fucking supposed to do? Clean up the act and marry a preacher?" Her eyes hold more intelligence than most. She's a survivor. "The guy you want to know about is more fucking fucked-up than a john. It still beats a preacher. At least he doesn't charge for stuff."

Hal kneels before the altar in The Sanctuary. He cleanses himself with fast, prayer, and meditation. In Hal's mind the black van is a dragon, and the murderer a demon. A demon rides a dragon. Hal prepares for battle, and his young face is serene. The handle of the sword rises as a cross behind his back. His blond hair glows. He prays to the Virgin Mary, and of course his prayer is answered. Hal understands the weakness of evil. He understands that those things which are unclean must always fall before those things which are holy.

The corpse of Maria Ramirez lies sodden in the rain. There is not much left. Small animals have taken the softest body parts, rain and decay take most of the rest. Already bones predominate above flesh, and eye sockets lie empty. Maria's black hair lies like a rain-battered wreath around her skull, and insects nest in the decay that fills her shoes. Weather has not treated her kindly, but she is not forgotten. Her killer has returned with ornaments. The bone that was once her ring finger has been gnawed clean, but not by the teeth of small animals. The marks carry the regularity of human teeth. A black ribbon is tied around the finger like a wedding ring. An elaborate black bow rests on what was once her chest. It is secured by ribbon passed beneath and around the corpse. Maria lies wrapped as a dark gift offered to a darkening world.

Traffic pulses, stops before stoplights, flows jerkily. Traffic jams up beside buses, and bus drivers remain phlegmatic as they ease huge vehicles from curb to driving lane. In a bus from the north end an old gentleman busily flips through canceled checks. A credit card statement accompanies the bank statement. The gentleman makes notes with an old-fashioned fountain pen. He attempts to chart a pattern of movement; at such-and-such-a-date the murderer was in the locale of a particular store, at such-and-such-a-date the murderer was at a different store in a different locale. It seems to the old gentleman that a circular pattern suggests itself. One month's statement is not much to go on. The old gentleman views the nature of purchases, but there seems no pattern. Then he mutters.

Canceled checks show dates when the checkwriter was far north in the city buying a set of tires, yet credit card charges for the same date show him downtown. A different signature endorses the charge slip. The writing is a woman's script. The old gentleman tsks, puzzles to himself, looks out the back window of the bus. A green XK-140 hovers in traffic. The bus approaches downtown. The old gentleman folds his notes and stuffs them in his pants pocket. He tucks the bank statement in his jacket.

Time to do the bunny hop, time to dance away from this mess. There's sure no time for transfiguration, just time for this old putz to get moving. The bus is about to arrive before a big department store, and there's no place better for hiding.

It's almost fun blending with the crowd. I follow a couple of black kids in their late twenties. They are man and woman, seriously in love. They dress better than Cosby, who they imitate. They're actually holding hands, and babies will come of this. I breathe a "God bless," as they descend, and then the guy turns to help me from the bus. The times they are achanging. Behind me an enormous fat man puffs white and racial. He doesn't like what he's seeing, but then, the poor slob cares for nothing but groceries. I thank the guy, and silently hope he does not take his new wife to a home in the black district. Get out while you can, my man. Your babies don't deserve life in the shadow of crackhouses. Before anything else, protect your family. Trust me, I've taught history.

The XK-140 dives for a parking garage as I putter my way into the department store. I've got a five-minute edge, ten at the outside. It's time to hide. There's an acre of women's wear and perfume to my left, a half acre of men's wear to my right. An escalator ripples like running water, but I'm a traditionalist. I'll camp right here on the main floor.

The floor buzzes with business as I head for men's wear. I'm looking for mannequins, and spot two good ones. One stands dressed in sport coat, pink shirt, and slacks. The other is seated. It wears golfing togs. I wear good wool and give a supercilious sniff while joining their little group. "Gentlemen," I say, "let me show you how to do this."

It's easy. Take a golf club and lean on it, facing kitty-corner to my golfing friends. Neutral lips. Concentrate on soft rock from a TV monitor which shows the Sebring road race. That causes the eyes to go neutral. I'm positioned to see most of the store. A little kid gawks at me, then tries to get his daddy's attention. Daddy fans a stack of polyester shirts and does not answer. The kid's attention span is not quite as long as a commercial. He looks elsewhere. Salesmen pass me without hesitation. No one cares for the opinions of mannequins.

Our killer is an actor, after all. He's not a very good actor, because he enters the store fast and walks fast while pretending to be casual. He has his right hand in his pants pocket. You can bet it's wrapped around a switchblade. He stops before a pile of sweats, pretending he's shopping while looking over the floor. He looks straight at me and sees nothing. His left hand rumples sweaters. It's a nervous hand. The guy isn't steady. That's hard to understand. If he's killed so many women, and if he's avoided being caught for so long, he should be steady.

The longer he stands the more agitated he gets. The TV monitor changes from soft rock and racing engines to Montovani and about a million violins. The monitor shows a guy dining with a doll, and the guy is obviously about to make it. He dresses well. Meanwhile, our murderer seems loaded with frustration. He quits diddling the sweaters and heads fast for the escalator. It's a good, wide escalator, but crammed with shoppers. I watch his back as tension twitches his shoulders. He's barely under control while being borne heavenward on moving stairs. He's starting to shake.

As he disappears an older lady tumbles backward with a scream. The escalator ripples with human dominoes, maybe a dozen people tumbling while carried upward. Lots of yelling going on. Our murderer lost his patience, and an old woman pays. I hope she's all right but have my doubts. People run, salesmen turn their attention to goods so nothing gets ripped off. There's a real brouhaha being dumped from the mouth of that escalator onto second floor. If no one's dead it's a miracle.

Time for graceful exit. My old gentleman has served the cause. Bless his gnarly old hide and heart. He was a patriot. I wish there were time to know him better. For now, there is only time to get on the street and to The Sanctuary.

ACT

FOUR

XV

It is a week of storms. In windows of used-appliance stores, television weathermen chirp like mechanical birds as they point to satellite photos of weather fronts rolling from the Aleutians. Wind and driving rain sweep Jericho with biblical vengeance. Teeney is dead. Maria is dead. Katie is on the street. Water rises in choked gutters. Cars stall. Drug dealing moves into bars. Winos find shelter in abandoned buildings, and fire erupts as flooring and woodwork are ripped apart and burned for heat. Fires color our world with crimson irony. Firemen lean against the pressure of hoses as rain washes their yellow slickers. The hoses pour crashing streams through rain. Occasionally a wino, or a runaway kid, dies from smoke inhalation. Some years a fireman does the same.

Meanwhile, the play continues. Already we come to the fourth act. This is an Elizabethan play. Five acts. Count them.

We sit, my friends and I, in the vestibule of The Sanctuary, and look through open doors onto the street. There'll be no sitting outside during evenings this week. This week the homosexual bar will flash pink above wet pavement. Jorge Ramirez will daily return home wet and shivering from the labor pool. He will towel himself, don dry clothes, prepare his evening search for Maria. Jorge has two rain slickers, both worn out. One dries before the face of the oven while he wears the other. For the past few nights he is joined in his search by Van Loon, who searches for Katie. The Dutchman and the Mexican are two tired figures disappearing into gloom; and one of them, Van Loon, carries a pistol.

Jericho, oh, Jericho—*And it shall come to pass that when they make a long blast with the ram's horn, and when ye hear the sound of the trumpet, all the people shall shout with a great shout; and the wall of the city shall fall down flat. . . . Joshua 6:5.*

I watch belov'ed Silk, iron-colored hair more Puritan than Romish. I see her dear face, lips compressed with worry, her eyes gentle with concern as she watches Elgin and Hal. Silk has not stood naked before the altar for many months. She changes. She—who was once the wife of Christ—now more resembles the Holy Mother of us all. She is our protector.

Still, she has no business inquiring about the murderer. She is a woman, and our murderer kills women. In protecting us she may be destroyed, and that will spill the batter. Our noble spirit Hal will seek revenge. The rest of us will fade.

Hal carries a calling horn fashioned from deer antler. Is that the same as a ram's horn? If not the same, will it serve?

Elgin watches pink glow on the street. "Gods of western storms wear beards of rain. They holler wind, belch clouds, old fat-gut gods of storm. We peep and cheep and advertise, while they scream in the tower. They be cacophonous. We're clangphony-ous."

"The shit is hitting the fan." Symptomatic Nerve Gas does not care that Elgin makes up new words, and would probably say we already have too many words. Symptomatic Nerve Gas presses to-ward action. He will argue that we have blown our advantage. We are no longer invisible street people. He will argue that the time to strike is *now*. "We'd better do something quick," he tells us. "You people screw up worse than Army intelligence."

"Put it all together," Elgin says about the murderer. "My wine-man in the red hat sees 'pretty mama.' With him, it never dresses as a man. Pretty momma don't leave news for ugly girls. It likes 'em gorgeous."

"What messages," I ask.

"Messages to meet." Elgin stares sadly toward pink puddles. "Pretty momma and the girls go shopping."

None of us are exactly stunned. At the same time, this is not what we expected. Our demon takes prostitutes on shopping trips?

"That's what he does," Silk says. "But it doesn't stop there. When he's a man he picks up girls in that van, and not all of those girls are pretty. All they do is talk." Her voice sounds like she can't believe what she says, even if she only reports what she's heard.

A dark pattern appears. Our demon is spectacular in its way. At the same time, things we already know fit a design. This Northwest has hosted fruitcakes. We have The Order, a group of Nazi cowards. We have endured the serial rapist Kevin Coe. We recoiled before the murders of Ted Bundy, who made Jack the Ripper look like a mewling baby. We have Skinheads who specialize in wolf-pack tactics, too yellow to stand alone. In small towns south of this city, a messianic type named Fred is the Charles Manson of animal mutilation. Cats drag themselves home, bellies slit and guts dangling. Horses are found decapitated in fields. If you wish to view darkness, look in private corners beneath our dark skies.

The serial murderer is not like an actor. An actor prepares. An actor enters into role with respect, even love, for the character. Theatre takes a man's loneliness, or uncertainty, and turns them to art. The serial murderer takes those same things and turns them to phantasmic forms of evil. The murderer can't get into role because its signals are all wrong.

The murderer Ted Bundy would not leave the house unless he had the correct running shoes. The rapist Kevin Coe stretched

123

yellow cellophane across his license plate so it would appear as a vanity plate. Mixed signals.

And so the pattern emerges. Our murderer picks up girls. He pays them to shop for stylish eyeglasses, cologne, makeup. He sends them on shopping sprees, and they buy things for him/her and for themselves. The murderer talks of winning lotteries, and asks the girls what they would do with a million dollars. The murderer talks about the right clothes for the Bahamas, consulting seriously with girls about points of wardrobe. The murderer knows every style, every brand name, every designer. It wistfully talks of becoming a rock star, and sometimes the murderer and the girls sing popular songs. Often the murderer is male, sometimes female; and the girls all agree he/she is kinky but harmless. The van is expensively decorated and has a bed, but girls who assume sex are dropped off right away. What the murderer wants is their opinion of deodorants, stylish gloves, vacation spots, sex changes, dancing slippers.

The nervous pattern also fits. Emptiness increases until space must be filled. Nerves clang. Only violence fills the void. John David Chapman did not shoot John Lennon because he hated him. He shot John Lennon because he loved him. For one sharp moment of mortality he became John Lennon.

We are uncertain.

"Take what we know to the police."

"There is not one shred of proof."

"Katie Van Loon is on the street."

"A lot of others, also."

We turn to Elgin. Surely Elgin knows. While it is generally a mistake to trust young poets, you can usually trust the old ones.

"Displace it into turmoil," Elgin says. "Toss hot biscuits. Let it play catch." Wrinkles around Elgin's eyes hold black shadows as pink flows on his forehead. He stands wrapped in an Army blanket, dark hands floating toward night as he gestures to the street. The vestibule stands as an architect's best shot, but wasted on the

Dutch. It more resembles a space beneath arches than it does a room. Darkness rests in those high arches. Faint and far away, demons shriek from the tower. "Our man sees the way of it," Elgin says about Symptomatic Nerve Gas. "Popcorn don't pop except with heat."

We understand. If our murderer collects himself, he will come after us. If we keep him frenzied long enough, he will make a mistake. There's no long-range strategy; this is pure tactics. We turn to Symptomatic Nerve Gas.

"Always protect the flank," he says. "Offense or defense makes no difference. You can't show a soft spot." Symptomatic Nerve Gas may despise war, but he understands soldiering. We feel better already.

Symptomatic Nerve Gas turns to Silk. "You and Elgin ain't out of this, but you're outta here." He turns to me. "Rent rooms at Cathedral Mansion. Elgin and Silk will stay there. I don't want 'em anywhere near this place."

Elgin's nose twitches, as if the nose thinks of smells from Cathedral Mansion; of canned beef stew heated on hotplates, of old men's armpits unwashed, the cocky smells of bikers. "How come we gotta move?"

"You *think* he don't know where you're at. He *knows*. All he has to do is ask around the street. One dumb guess and you're grease."

"This had better be good," Silk tells him. She looks toward Hal, and her voice lowers. "Saint Jude, aid us. Saint Theresa, we are a family here."

Symptomatic Nerve Gas turns to Hal. "Quit starving yourself. You're going to need your strength."

Hal stands in darkness like a pure spirit. High arches are like frames presenting him as a cameo most noble. The hilt of the sword rises at his back, the shape of the Holy Cross he follows is a positive shadow behind his face. "I've cleansed with fast and prayer," he says. "It's fit that in this storm a demon rides. Winds of Heaven roar beside my arm. My sword is blessed. We'll match it storm for storm."

"You're a good kid, but you talk dumb." Symptomatic Nerve Gas stands in the doorway of The Sanctuary. He looks toward Cathedral Mansion. "He'll come here first, but he won't come in. He'll have learned that other people live here." Symptomatic Nerve Gas turns to Hal. "You pull guard. As long as he can see you he won't mess with this place. He'll wait for Elgin and Silk. If he makes one move toward Cathedral Mansion take him out."

Silk begins to object. Elgin touches her arm, shakes his head. Elgin understands our demon isn't likely to find them at Cathedral Mansion. Elgin knows that Hal is given the assignment most likely to keep him out of battle.

"I'll relieve you from time to time. You'll have to get some sleep."

"Don't demean," Hal says. "The watchful eye of God will no more close than mine."

He tells the truth. Hal carries his mandate from Heaven. He will not sleep though he watches for a week.

Symptomatic Nerve Gas turns to me. "We have some thinking to do."

"There's a role I've always wanted to try," I tell him. "I've been preparing it for a lifetime. Give me three hours. We'll talk."

XVI

The sacristy holds my monkish bed where Silk will never visit. A kerosene lamp throws soft glow into the room. On one side of me lies my trumpet. On the other side is a Bible. It's nice to sit between things that, in the right hands, can come alive. Old-time prophets understood such things, but then, so does the Salvation Army.

The role I prepare is complex, largely because parts of it are parts of me. I'll tend to slip out of it more quickly. This will take a lot of concentration.

The role is a fifty-four-year-old man who is a jack-of-all-trades. As a young man he spent a couple of years studying to be a preacher. He got booted out of divinity school because his balls were tingly. He could not stay away from women. He went to sea for four years, then drove big trucks. He left the road to work as a gardener. He drifted from gardening into a government job. That lasted about eighteen months, then, exhausted with bureaucracy, he ran away and joined the circus. The circus he joined was not really a circus. It was a carnival; but in his memories he likes to pretend he was a circus trumpeter. In reality he was a pitchman. He loved the crowds, the showmanship, the ability to bend desire toward ringtoss or hoochy-koochy.

Then for awhile he worked in stables teaching horsemanship to little kids. After that he worked on a weekly newspaper where he reported high school football games, City Council meetings, and the numbers of DWI convictions in county court. He married a few times, but the marriages were more stormy than the sea. He *liked* women for their breasts and their strange ways of viewing the obvious. He *loved* women for their practicality, and for their propensity to storm. His marriages crashed on rocks, but the rocks were spectacular.

These days he gets his living hustling pool. My role is more sinner than saint, but there's a streak of saintliness in him somewhere. As he ages, and his balls shrink, the saintly part increases.

Also, I like the way he looks. He affects an expensive suit and string tie. His shirts are white. He takes pride in never having a spot of cue chalk on his shirt. His hair is too long to match his outfit, and hair curls in wisps around his head. On the pool circuit, where everyone has a name, he is known as "The Preacher." In this city few hustlers remain. They are Shi Shi John, Sasquatch, Peanut Louise, Jaybird George, and Issaquah Pete. The Preacher gets his name because he constantly analyzes his game with quotes from scriptures.

And now, it is time to try on the role.

This gentleman I'm working with, Symptomatic Nerve Gas, is no doubt able, but may be too direct. We require a subtle hand, not a doctored cue ball.

I sit in a pew in The Sanctuary waiting for him to appear. Darkness hovers. Darkness clusters in the choir. We will surely have some theater develop here, although the place is poorly designed for action.

It was built in 1901, but for all intents was planned in 1840. In that year something called the Ecclesiological Movement rose in Europe. A hymnologist named Neale figured the Gothic cathedrals of the Middle Ages showed the only correct way to build a church. What came of his notions were buttresses, high arches, steep roofs. There are towers and pointed windows of stained glass. There's a far-too-narrow central aisle on the axial plan, plus a deep chancel. The chancel is cleanly set off from the nave by a divided choir.

This style lasted for a hundred years. The design causes great depths of darkness. That fits with the Middle Ages. That fits with demons.

The stage, however, is cluttered. Pews run in continuous lines, with only the central aisle breaking them (although there are side aisles along the walls). It resembles a badly designed movie theater. Choir lofts are high-walled so only heads of the choir might be seen from the floor, and the floor itself is slanted. The pulpit is a monster in dark mahogany, the font is too big. Pipes of the organ rise above the choirs, and before the choirs stand altar table and communion rail. There is a lectern, while the presider's chair is really a short pew. It is no wonder Silk and Hal feel comfortable here. This place may be Dutch Protestant, but one could say a mass without trouble.

Religion is not so different from billboards. Both require focus, geometric purity, physics, and—if a pun may be forgiven—absolute gravity. There's also a certain amount of aerodynamics. Properly cued, a ball actually floats. The same may be the case with angels.

Symptomatic Nerve Gas approaches. Young Hal walks beside him. I fear for Hal. He may be the last pure spirit of this world. At the same time, he has been on the street for several years and remains uncorrupted.

"We'll do it this way. We have to stop him before he kills another one." Symptomatic Nerve Gas is already getting "up" for a fight. His puffy lips compress, and large-knuckled hands clench in loose fists. He is not agitated, but cannot relax enough to sit. "We decoy him out of his house, or out of the van. We get him to go after one guy, while the other guy catches him blindside. Bend a tire iron over his head, call the cops, let him explain those knives. If he's crazy as you say, he'll make a mistake when the cops question him."

It is not a bad plan. It is simple and direct. It is also necessary, because the demon could kill again at any time. However, there's one uncertainty. "You assume the police will be interested," I say sadly. "They won't."

Silence. Symptomatic Nerve Gas thinks about it. Police suffer the same sorrows as most bureaucrats, which is to say they have no imagination. They still search for a man and not a demon.

"The way to snooker someone," I suggest, "is provide hope and focus, while dividing his attention. Let him think he wins as he digs himself into trouble. Matthew 27:64: 'so the last error shall be worse than the first.' "

"This guy can't think in a straight line. How can you snooker him?" Symptomatic Nerve Gas must know something about pool.

"You snooker his feelings, not his logic. He's a consumer. Perhaps we should advertise."

"I understand advertising," Hal says. "To clothe a deceit in the vestments of truth, so that by its raiment you shall believe it equal to that which is good."

Hal may be a monomaniac, but he is no fool.

"Let's try this," I say. "Symptomatic Nerve Gas and I will find the wino in the red hat. We'll stand near him and gossip. After a few minutes I'll mention a rumor. I'll say I've heard of this lad in the black van, and that he has won a trip to Florida. Along with the prize comes an appearance on television."

It's a pleasure to see Symptomatic Nerve Gas this pleased. "That takes our guy off the street," he says. "The damn fool will be afraid to leave home. He'll sit beside the phone. He might miss his prize."

"He'll get the phone call." I am nigh hopeful. This plan might just work. "We have to do something quick before he kills again. No matter how it falls out, it has to happen quickly."

In the street cars plash, are rocked with wind channeling

through alleys and around buildings. Jericho gets cleansed. The original Jericho fell because it was impotent. It had only its walls for defense. It had no strength of purpose. It could not defend its children.

"We have two problems," I say. "We need keep him contained so he presents no threat to another woman, and especially no threat to Silk. We also have a long-range problem. We have to figure a way for him to betray himself to the police. Police being who they are, we must get him to make his mistake under their very noses."

"If we wind our skein with passions," Hal predicts, "the untoward may happen. I fear mischance."

I'll wager Hal knows nothing of hustling, but he's correct. Emotions complicate things. This killer is a catastrophe of emotions. Too much gets left to luck. As we all know, there are two kinds of luck.

"Rule number one. Never hit a cop." Symptomatic Nerve Gas has the directness we need.

"Getting him to hit a policeman is a very good plan." I say this almost sadly because a grand notion comes to mind. In my scheme there are lights and TV cameras and police cars and music and people dancing. Everything is comic. I think in terms of Danny Kaye, while Symptomatic Nerve Gas thinks of Brando. We'll try his way first. If that doesn't work, we'll try mine.

One simple way is to file a theft report on the killer's XK-140. My role can do that. Then, the role can convince our killer that *It* will be taped for television. We'll make a daytime appointment for It at a studio. Then I'll call the police and tell them the stolen car will pass a certain intersection at a certain time. The police will arrest him for stealing his own car. He will be so frenzied at missing his chance for television he'll do something ungainly. If we can raise his frustration high enough beforehand, he'll make a really bad miscue.

It's such an easy layout I'm nearly afraid. I turn to Symptomatic Nerve Gas. "Let's go plant the rumor now. He'll hear it on the street tonight. I'll phone tomorrow. Proverbs 11:3: '. . . the perverseness of transgressors shall destroy them.'" To Hal, I say, "Watch-keeping is tedious duty, but important." I say this kindly, because my plan gives me a small feeling of power.

Then I recall that Hal has kept watch over the parks and neighborhoods of this city, watched over schoolchildren and women and old people. He does not even deign to answer.

XVII

The street is washed with rain and morning light. Last night we planted the rumor. This morning I leave a police station after a splendid performance. My lower lip actually trembled as I reported the theft of my treasured XK-140. It's a credit to me. I detest automobiles, because I've driven trucks.

This early in the day my umbrella is the only one bobbing along this street. Doors of missions stand closed, and inside men and women and children chew on reconstituted scrambled eggs before their day on the street. Out here in the street men huddle beneath canopies where the day labor pool assembles. Some are hungover, but most are like Jorge Ramirez: poor fellows with families, doing the best they can. I find love in my heart for such men, little but scorn for the people who hire them. Jorge Ramirez was doomed from birth by his Mexican passivity.

To be charitable, though, maybe fat cats are also doomed. It must be terrible to live with all bustle, no hustle. These days men do not trade horses or swap knives, they roll over investment accounts.

I walk, thinking of our murderer. *It*, the demon, is not so atypical. Any hustler could figure It out, just from what Silk and Elgin have to say. When It is a male he picks up any girl, even ugly ones. When female she picks up only pretty girls. It apparently doesn't bed any of them. Once in a while, for reasons unknown, It chooses to murder with knives. This demon is strictly swine, but not that unusual. This demon is homegrown.

It's a consumer, and there is where the greatest horror lies. We've created the ultimate consumer. When in the male role our demon consumes women. Female throwaways. Our demon is not doing a thing that commerce, on some level, has not told it to do. It's getting the big laugh on a world where actors in TV commercials become famous as Presidents.

I've a responsibility in this. I have a bit of power to change the situation, because there's power in theater. I can't change the demon, but can help catch him.

When in the female role *she's* in competition with Cinderella, or with those TV Cinderellas who sell douche or soap. She's programmed. She's logical, given the circumstances. The female role kills the pretty girls, and you can wager the female role killed Teenie.

Micah 5:15: "And I will execute vengeance in anger and fury...."

Vengeance against whom? This monster is our creation—God forgive me—*my* creation. I've been the talent before the lights. I've used sex to sell cornbread mix and airline tickets. I helped raise the sleaze ratio. I've snookered millions with illusions. Who, now, is the one who's snookered?

There's more than one way to snooker. A very good way is to allow your man to believe he's snookering you. The easiest person to hustle is another hustler.

Another way is to throw him into confusion, and there's nothing more confusing than a mixture of good and bad. I walk thinking of ways to work on this demon's mind.

The first move asks that he be convinced of a legitimate prize and a real TV appearance. If there is a flaw it will show up when I phone him. However, if he follows the pattern of other serial killers, he will be an easy sell. These killers are so absorbed with their images they are compelled to focus attention on themselves. More than any other condition, they wish for the limelight. . . .

Thinking about this scam, I slip out of role. It's hard to understand why any sap would want to be on television. Yet, at every football game, when the camera pans the crowd, fans crush each other in an attempt to get on camera. Television holds the fascination of magic. It offers instant fame to people who feel they are nonentities.

I slip back into role. It's easy to slip out, but fairly easy to slip back in.

The second move asks us to raise this demon's ambivalence. If all goes well during the phone call, I'll follow up by sending flowers addressed to the female side of the demon. I'll include a note reading, "From an admirer." Since we're unsure what mental aberrations are involved, flowers may make the male side jealous. Or, they may do nothing, or they may make him proud. Odds are they'll tweak his insecurity. They certainly tweak mine. Flowers make me uneasy.

The third move asks that I work on his fears. We have newspaper photos of the dead girls. Maybe I'll enclose two or three in an envelope and have them delivered by courier.

These opening moves should be sufficient. If our scheme fails it may be necessary to work up something really nasty.

Meanwhile, it's time for breakfast. In two hours offices open for business. If I phone too early our demon will suspect fraud. There's time for a leisurely meal.

In this area coffee shops peddle croissants beside hash houses slinging soggy eggs. I pick a hash house because it carries no pretensions. A seat beside the window allows me to watch the street awake, and offers a chance to treat with my fellow creatures. Luke

24:15: "And it came to pass, that, while they communed together and reasoned...."

This restaurant is a comfort. It has surely been here since the 1930s, and has changed in no large way. A coffee urn steams as cigarette smoke forms blue layers in the air. The grill also smokes, and photographs along the walls are dimmed with smoke. This was once a tugboatman's café. Photos show tugs of every variety, from the little sixty-four-footers through the hundred and tens through the two-hundred-foot oceangoing tugs. I am no more fond of yachts than of sports cars. Give me a tugboat or a truck every time.

The restaurant must have been established about the year I was born, 1935. I do not know if birth years form restaurants, but sure as ducks they form men. Why would anyone born in '35 not be a hustler? Hustling is the way we preserve our ideals....

Something is about to happen. There's a sense a man develops when he's worked in the circus. The circus depends on the balancing of a thousand different things, from the mood of a performer to the smallest bolt in the rigging. I've got the same feeling that used to come when everyone knew something was out of balance, but no one knew where to look.

I view the restaurant. Two retired men sit at one end of the counter reading newspapers. A slattern sits at a table and mumbles seriously to her coffee cup. At the other end of the counter a couple of delivery men chomp donuts. They talk about women and bowling.

My waitress is a tall Korean with muted voice. She fumbles English as unsteadily as a three-year-old stacking wooden blocks. I give her a brotherly smile, order breakfast, and compliment her on her use of language. She shies from the compliment like a startled mare. The cook darts, flips eggs and pancakes. He is small and black. The counterman is Middle Eastern. He could be Jordanian, or a son of Levi.

The Nineties already resemble the Thirties in at least one way. There's a lot of hatred. In the Thirties this country hated Jews and Negroes and Catholics. When war arrived in '41 hatred widened to include Japanese, Germans, Italians. Anyone born in '35 was raised on more hatred than was ever taught to Nazi youth. It gave us a real enemy to fight.

Hustling preserves the spirit because it helps one understand the human condition. Hustlers live by the cupidity of others, teaching humility to those who want to frame a few fast bucks. Hustling is antisocial. After a few years it becomes spiritual. Acts 3:16: "... faith ... hath given him this perfect soundness."

Television putters on the back bar, and now I see where trouble will come from. A news anchor pulls her "this-is-terribly-serious" look. This particular flack makes her reputation by appearing wholesome. At present she looks like Doris Day playing Lady Macbeth, Jell-O with acrimony.

"I don't know how much more of this people can endure." She says this to her fellow news anchor. This particular flack makes his reputation as contrast. At present he looks like Stallone in *Leave It to Beaver*, like he's got a diaper full of crap and is proud.

They've really yanked me out of role. Way out of role.

Two photos appear on the screen. One is a young woman whose corpse has just been discovered in the north end of town. The other is Maria Ramirez, a second discovery. The photos show young innocence, while the male flack reports police opinion that both were tied to prostitution.

"And now this ... ," says a flack. An actress with big knockers begins to sell styles for "full-figured" females. A Jane Russell recording honks in the background.

Grief washes over me with original fury. I knew Maria was dead, but until now the fact was part of the play. I could perform around the fact, hold death as a necessary element of drama. Now, with the sanction of police and television, the death is real.

On some level I'm insane, which means I'm more crazy than everyone else. I should know better. Maria's death was death all along. Consequences on the street will be real.

Silk and Elgin are no longer safe. The plan to keep them at Cathedral Mansion is busted. Silk will leave the hotel. There is not a chance in the world Silk will stay away from the Ramirez family. Silk is wise. She will know they cannot be comforted, but she will bring more comfort than will their priest. Silk will do her best.

Elgin's nose will command him onto the street. Elgin is tribal. He cannot sit safely at Cathedral Mansion while the tribe suffers wounds. I can already feel the depth of Elgin's grief, feel his metaphors of sorrow sailing like black kites in the mist.

I do not know what young Hal will do, except that he will do his duty. It is more desperately important than ever that we distract the murderer. I *have* to take that guy off the street. I *must*. If this scam doesn't work, I've got another; and it will work because I've just realized something.

Television makes real that which is unreal, and vice versa. At the same time it authenticates situations. It makes a suspicion seem to be a fact. If the murderer stands accused on television, the police will take the accusation as seriously as will everyone else. If this fails, we've still got a real way out. I'll return to television. My mind rebels at the idea, but by the Lord Harry I'll do it. I know exactly how.

The waitress places breakfast before me. Her face remains impassive, but eyes show pain and fear. Perhaps she has daughters. At the far end of the counter the two retired men complain in muted voices of how the world has changed; and those old voices also echo fear. The cook lowers the sound on the television, then spreads bacon across the grill. His back seems suddenly limp, and he stands above the grill like a small, black question. The counterman rolls his eyes, mutters beneath his breath.

Something more will happen. I don't know what. I'm out of role, my mind leathery as these fried eggs on my plate.

The delivery men discuss pistols. Their hatred churns with ignorance and purity. They would deliver the world of murderers, and would do it with guns. We all turn as the slattern rises to prophesy.

She is one of us, a woman of the street. She is one of our least creatures, lost in madness or monomania. This particular lady is not old. Perhaps she is mid-thirties, but with ages and ages of torment resting on slumped and rounded shoulders. Her hair hangs stringy beneath a wool sock hat, her figure dumpy in workshirt and floor-length skirt. Her shoes do not match, and one is nearly new. Shopping bags rest beside her chair.

"Kings of Wrath," she says to someone or something no more than twelve inches in front of her eyes. Great privacy lives in this encounter. She stands among us, but she is all alone, her voice a rising storm. "And the people shall come to a *mighty* river, and the torrent shall *sweep,* oh Lord, and the torrent shall bear away the children." Her eyes still focus on something twelve inches before her face. Her voice strengthens, and there is only anger, no hysteria. "And trumpets of *Wrath* and the Kings of *Wrath* shall deliver them across the flood, and caravans of camels and horses bearing silks will furnish raiment for their final day." Hers is the voice of fury.

"And yet will the *skies* then open, and the earth become a howling wound, and will not the earth open and swallow them silken clad to sullen depths of fire. And the people will cry not for *children* of the torrent, but will wail and cover their unholiness. . . ."

The waitress is by her side, the cook darting around the end of the counter. The counterman stands rapt, as if he is slaughtered with truth; and the delivery men blush and mumble. They leave money on the counter, and nearly race each other to the street. The retired men sit mute, look at each other, nod as if affirming madness.

"You got it right, my Susie," the cook says. "You got it pat. You be okay in a minute, 'cause you got it certified." He stands beside Susie but does not touch her. The great privacy of the woman radiates about her slumped figure. She pants, sweats, trembles; but she is alone and wishes it that way. The cook makes soothing noises.

Such great love is nearly more than I can bear. All of us are wounded, yet some attend the wounds of others. I rise, nearly staggering, leave money on the table.

*   *   *

The street echoes wind and rain. I huddle beneath a canopy a half block from the restaurant. Traffic presses against a new storm winging in from the Aleutians. Brake lights pop. Headlights flare. Traffic lights command us. This day is filled with bruises.

I'm not yet struggling to get back into role. I struggle for normal breath. The chest is tight, I wolf at air. The feeling that something more will happen does not pass. I wait for the next evil thing. It is a short wait.

The murderer's black van rises in traffic a block away. Traffic is stop-and-go. The van proceeds slowly. Painted demons on the van have faces washed with rain. Beneath this darkened sky the van regains ominous appearance. It may look tawdry in daylight, but this dark morning gives substance to darkness.

I stand unthinking. It's enough to watch, to take in horror. As the van comes alongside it brakes behind traffic. Painted demons rise from painted pools of blood. The decorations are active, the blood not stagnant; the faces of demons twist and hiss through rain. Windows are rolled, impossible to see inside. The driver is impatient. The van rocks against its brakes, jolts forward, rocks against its brakes. He's almost running into other cars. What is the murderer doing on the street in morning rush hour? The murderer is a creature of the night.

Is the murderer headed for The Sanctuary? Helplessness comes howling. Here I am, out of role, too choked for action. Hal waits at The Sanctuary. Dear young Hal. He has never seen such evil as this which putters its exhaust before me. I imagine the bed in that van, imagine a blood-soaked young woman lying violated with knives.

The driver's impatience seems monstrous. The van rocks forward, stops. This thing, this murderer, is foul. It tramples all decency, then protests when stuck in traffic.

The van nears the curb and blocks a driving lane. Auto horns rise, but the driver pauses contemptuous. The door on the rider's side opens and Katie Van Loon slips out. She jumps across a puddle, tennis shoes slipping on wet sidewalk. She is quick. I stand amazed. Katie runs through the rain without fear. She dashes to avoid the weather. At the end of the block her squarish form disappears through the doorway of a flophouse. No doubt she is already lost to us, but in a way she is also found. At least I know where she hides.

I turn away, heading back to sanctuary, then turn back again as scorching tires burn against wet streets. Harsh sounds of tearing metal and broken glass erupt as the black van clears the intersection. Our murderer jumped the light, and now there's a collision; but he's not in it. This bastard deals in wreckage.

XVIII

The street fills with lamentation, and demons chortle in the bell-tower. Silk sits with the Ramirez family. The wives of Van Loon and Vandermeer are earnest women who bring earnest Dutch cooking to Mexicans. Katie Van Loon's mother trundles steaming bowls. She walks with fear because Katie is on the street. She allows herself hope because I have told Van Loon where Katie hides. Van Loon is not our friend—at least he doesn't like me—but he heads for the flophouse to retrieve Katie. On the street, city work crews put up plastic decorations for Mardi Gras: plastic flowers and plastic fat men, very jolly. I sit in The Sanctuary and struggle back into role.

"We must crack the whip and do so immediately," I say to Symptomatic Nerve Gas.

"Where the hell is Elgin?" Symptomatic Nerve Gas stands beside me. His lips are purplish with pulse and anger. He does not see this as theatre, and he does not understand the power of drama. The man believes my "play-acting" the indulgence of a madman.

"You might well ask from whence the wind," Hal says. "Elgin walks in mourning."

"We'll walk his scrawny can into a trap. That killer will dress him out like pork."

"We'll make certain that doesn't happen." There is no time for me to explain how sharkishness now enters the picture. In sports it is called "the killer instinct," and perhaps that is an adequate term. There comes a moment in any hustle when no mistakes are allowed. You have to wreck the opponent. I do not like it much, but must confess to being adept. Daniel 5:21: ". . . and his heart was made like the beasts. . . ."

"You can't help Elgin," I say to Hal. "You can watch over Silk and the Ramirez house. Let no one enter who you do not know. If matters become untidy we'll bring everyone to Sanctuary."

"Elgin can't be far. There's too much rain." Symptomatic Nerve Gas is too tense for this maneuver. Best get him out of the way.

"You search for Elgin," I tell him, and check my watch. It is nearly ten A.M. "We'll meet back here this evening. If you find Elgin, persuade him he's needed here. That won't be hard because it's true."

I'll operate from Cathedral Mansion, because at Cathedral Mansion money buys anything a poor place has to sell. Right now I need time on two telephones.

The lobby is small, and to the right is a large dayroom with television, a couple of video games, and a sweet old Brunswick pool table only a little smaller than Noah's ark. A couple of old gents shoot nine-ball, and wait to hustle bikers. These gaffers have been shooting the same game for thirty years, learning nothing new; and while they can trim these biker kids with great dexterity, I'd find them too easy. TV broadcasts soap. It appears someone's gynecologist has been kissing unborn babies. "I won't say it wasn't exciting,

Madge," an actress sobs. "Just a little *too* unusual." Madge coos and makes worry sounds.

Two misers, male and female, own Cathedral Mansion. They are married to the place and to each other. The old man has varicose veins in his earlobes. The old woman has a voice made scratchy by a half century of bawling out Chinese and Puerto Rican chambermaids. A two-dollar tip would buy this place.

There's a phone at the desk, and a phone in their apartment. I rent both for the day. The old man closes doors to the dayroom. I need no click of balls or tinkle of video to interrupt my performance.

Our murderer answers on the third ring, his voice neutral but sleepy. I confirm his name, confirm that he bought four tires for a sports car.

"This is Purity Productions," I say with just the right amount of hype. "We're doing a TV promo called 'American Classics.' You put those tires on an old Jag?"

He admits he did.

"What shape is it in?"

He swears it's perfect.

"You picked the right tires," I tell him. "The company wants ads from across the country, classic cars and their owners. We pay you for the spot, and our client gives you a week at Daytona."

My mark pauses. He actually gasps. Still, he's cautious.

"Do it," I tell him. "The only other lead I've got is an Aston Martin we have to paint. A week's delay."

"I'll get back to you," our killer says. "Name and number."

I give him name and number, and tell him Purity Productions is a subsidiary of an international trust. I wait. He'll call back in twenty minutes. Right now he's looking up Purity Productions in his phone book. He won't find it, but he will find the international trust. Odds are better than even he'll call the trust. It's so big someone will either confirm ownership of Purity, or else will say they think the trust owns it. People who answer phones like to sound important. They'll talk about "doing lunch" even when carrying a brown bag with cold cuts.

The scam works. He calls back in twenty-one minutes. I put on a phone operator's voice, telling him the number he's called has been changed. Then I move to the other telephone. I answer in a secretary's voice. Then I come back with my hustler's voice, apologizing when he complains about the bum phone number. "Installing a new system. Glad you got around it."

I've got this sucker hooked. He's almost breathless. I make a date for tomorrow morning, and tell him not to get a haircut; our makeup people will handle how he looks. I tell him to detail the Jag. That will keep him off the street. This monkey has been up all night talking about bobby socks with Katie Van Loon. Now he must spend the day detailing that car. He'll sleep tonight.

I'll call him twice more today, to make sure he stays in place. From here on it's a matter of standing watch over the phone. He'll call back at least once. I'll be here to allay fears and confirm schedule. Habakkuk 2:3: "For the vision *is* yet for an appointed time, but at the end it shall speak. . . ."

The dayroom of Cathedral Mansion looks onto the street. Any hustler has to know how to loaf until situations firm. Some years ago, and south of here in a hot poolroom, I dropped seven games without getting a shot; fudged the shot, and dropped three more. Then the situation firmed and it was lights out in Roseville, Oregon. Timber haulers there no doubt recall the event. Their tickets carried a stately price.

The street looks like billiards played by ten-year-olds. There's much smashing and dashing and crashing. It partly comes from an influx of orientals. The poor dears can't drive because they're Buddhists. They don't believe two objects cannot occupy the same space at the same time.

At exactly 12:07 I phone our killer, speaking an artificial rap from script as I push a real estate scam. The irony pleases me, and my voice is that of a businesswoman with an MBA. The killer hangs with me for nearly two minutes because of the voice. He's not yet killed anyone with an MBA. No doubt he has fantasies.

At 12:47 Katie Van Loon passes by the window, accompanied by her father. Van Loon appears chastened, so does Katie. Perhaps experience teaches both to step more carefully. Maybe Katie has her fill of the street, and thank you, Lord. A couple of bikers loaf between games. They give thumbs-up and rub their crotches as Katie passes. She does not look through the windows of Cathedral Mansion.

At 1:30 I order flowers for the female side of our killer. It's a hurry-hurry phone call, most urgent. The merchant promises delivery before closing time. I use the killer's credit card number. Rain increases in the street. I imagine flowers; and shudder.

At 2:18 the killer calls back. He's still nearly breathless, muttering laudatory things about himself. I answer in a secretary's voice, then come back as the hustler. My mark asks questions about wardrobe. "It's an English car," I tell him. "Make it tweeds." The mark tries to be casual, gets around to the real reason for his call. Does he need an agent? Our killer is romping through fantasy land. By now he constructs his new television career. "Standard equity," I tell him. "Most agents won't frick with it, but you can try." This town is full of agents. I give him names of three firms. It's time to set the hook. "You get around," I say. "Research came up with a Maserati east of the lake. Know anything about it?"

He swears there isn't a Maserati in the whole Northwest. He's nicely scared. This plum could be picked by another car owner. I've taken him off adrenalin and onto anxiety. If he continues on adrenalin he might override fatigue and hit the street.

"Get a good night's rest," I tell him. "Filming is harder work than you think."

That old Brunswick table takes a beating. Bikers believe their pool cue is their wanger. They shoot only one way, and that's hard. These sullen youth lost drug money to the old geezers all day, and now the geezers run scared. Taunts of "old man" and "grandpa" become more frequent. Things could take an ugly turn. I'll make one more phone call just before five. A couple hours can be used for healing.

"You have to establish your game," I tell one of the punks. This particular drug dealer has teeth broken in his fight with Van Loon. "Right now you don't have a game." Authority in my voice makes him blink.

A seventeen-ounce cue is too light for gentle work, but it's the best the house has to offer. My own cue is nineteen-and-one-quarter-ounce, narrow taper and weighted butt. My breaking cue is an eighteen, because in bar pool it's hard to break clean with a heavy cue. All you do is slam them.

This is a friendly table. The left side of the rail on the breaking end is a trifle slack. There's slight table roll an inch-and-an-eighth along the right side, while one pocket sits slaunchwise a sixteenth of an inch. I've learned this table while watching it trick these drug-gers. "Keep racking," I say. One of the geezers' eyes go wide. He nudges the other geezer. Reputations are strange things. They run ahead of you, and suddenly you're a legend.

I run four racks in twelve minutes without missing a shot. Any-one who knows his way around a table doesn't have hard shots. The biker-punks know enough to suspect they watch mastery. Since they've never heard the word, leave alone observed a master, they're having a religious experience.

"Go back to school," I tell them, and lay a shot up the rail past the side pocket. "Physics teaches that a rotating object transfers op-posite rotation when striking another object." I cue six more up the right rail. Low-right English spins the cue ball left, and the left spin transfers to right spin. The object ball hugs the rail. Eighty-five percent of shots do not require English, but I can't take English away from them. Half of their shallow reach—if an insult may be forgiven—comes from how they spin their balls.

We commune for two enjoyable hours, and the punks get more instruction than they've received in their lives. They're actually learning something they want to learn. The excitement makes them nearly human. They wish to practice instead of beating on the geezers. Thus, do I offer my work of goodness for this day. First-Corinthians 8:1: "Knowledge puffeth up, but charity edifieth."

At 4:55 I call our murderer. With a teenager's voice I tell him my name is Liza, and I'm looking for my girlfriend Katie. Our murderer's adrenalin has run out. He mutters and seems confused. He asks where I got his phone number, but I won't tell. There's enough threat in that to give him bad dreams.

I leave Cathedral Mansion beneath a setting sun obscured by clouds. The entire universe is made up of various-sized balls. The whole blamed thing's a galactic game of snooker.

XIX

As night lies weightily on the street we gather in the vestibule of
The Sanctuary. Silk has her doubts about what we are attempting.
She stays close to Hal. They whisper to each other. Elgin remains
missing, and poetry departs from our world. We will not do well
without it. Symptomatic Nerve Gas is wordless. Dim light glows
through dusty windows of the Soft Porn Grocery. Vandermeer's
Great Dane woofs, and the red eyes of Vandermeer's security system shine vivid as small fires of Hell. The truck axle company has
not been robbed for quite some time. Its aluminum and sheet metal
façade reflect headlights. The poodle above the homosexual bar
seems covered with pink fuzz. The joint is quiet, seems paused
before Mardi Gras. Rain stops as fog descends.

   And, high above us in the belltower, demons chortle. Demons
stretch leathery wings across this city. They laugh at all of us.

In the north end the killer slumps before a television. The killer
exudes a faint odor of automobile polish. Fatigue relaxes its shoulders, and the killer reaches inside its nightgown to gently manipu-

late a small nipple on a small breast. Its other hand rests in a crotch most strangely fashioned; not exactly male, but not exactly female. A large spray of flowers stands on the television. On the television screen cops save orphan girls, shoot fallen women; and television lawyers flourish courtroom antics. Commercials flare, and, as the camera shows an expensive car at high speed, the killer's body stiffens, arches, trembles; then relaxes. It breathes heavily for moments, then lowers the skirt of its gown. It turns off sound on the television and removes to its bed. A sheath knife lies beneath its pillow, and the killer hugs the knife to its body as a child might sleep with a teddy bear. Snores begin, and darkness in the room stutters before flickering of the silent TV screen.

The street awakes with neon. In a nearby office building an executive works overtime. His hair is styled and tinted, his suit holds its press; and his eyes narrow in concentration. He engages in the great task of his life. He has been given the suppository account. If he comes up with an ad campaign—aggressive but in good taste—that moves these puppies out the door, it means a vice-presidency and 100K a year. If he doesn't, it's oblivion.

Katie Van Loon sits on her own bed in her own room. She has so many emotions she could kindle flames. The safety of home surrounds her, and she wonders why she ever left. Her dad has made no accusations. Her mother cried, and her mother never did that before. They must really like her after all. They must be getting smarter.

On the other hand, there are nice people on the street. There are some who are real shits, but you can find the nice ones. Katie spreads fifteen ten-dollar bills on the bed. She is supposed to shop for sweaters. One sweater is for the man who gave her the money, the other is for herself. If she does not keep her end of the deal the man will be mad.

There ought to be a way where you could live at home and go to school but still have special friends. She does not think her mom and dad have gotten smart enough to understand that. Katie sits trying to plan, but draws a blank. Tomorrow she will go to school. After school she'll go shopping. In a vague way she tells herself that everything will work out.

In the south end two cops respond to a possible break-in. The doorway of a darkened house stands open. They enter and turn on the lights. Neighbors gather in the yard. There is no break-in. Someone forgot to lock his door. The cops stand scratching their heads while swearing. Two automatic weapons lie on a bed. A small assortment of drugs clutter a coffee table. Any move the cops make constitutes illegal search and seizure. They stand helpless.

The street is filled with secret sleeping places. Bag ladies nest in basements of shuttered buildings. Men spread bindles in railway freight cars. These are the old pros of the street who know there are a thousand places to sleep safe and almost warm—the fun house at the amusement park—school buses—abandoned cars—toolsheds—beneath careened boats.

Those who are new to the street make mistakes. Women and children huddle before ventilators outside buildings, or in soggy cartons that once contained refrigerators. Teenagers cling together for warmth behind restaurants. They wait for food scraps to hit the dumpsters. Men huddle in the concrete restrooms of the parks.

In the entry to a thrift store a wino is down and headed for detox, if he's lucky. Two attendants from 911 check pulse and respiration. A faded red hat lies on the sidewalk like a worn pink tongue. One attendant shakes his head. He is young and angry. The other attendant is a gray-haired man who works quickly and well. He is fatalistic, and old enough to know the odds.

Elgin's nose has placed him outside the main library which is about to close. Elgin sniffs the mist for poems. In the library, volumes of poetry stand shelved and largely unread. From the library's hearth of central heating and fluorescent lights, it seems that at least a few poems should wander into this darkness, rising airily to conflict with demons. Elgin murmurs the name of Maria Ramirez—may angels wave their ghostly wings and bring her home. There is no scent of poetry, although high above in the gray mist rise shrieks of arcane laughter.

Elgin's nose swings him slowly around. He trudges into the mist, looking like a lost child in a world of lost children; but that is deceptive. Elgin is not lost, and Maria's death has finally pressed him into action.

"We joust with hidden dangers." Hal stares into fog toward the homosexual bar. "May God forfend. I fear ill chance." He reaches above his shoulder to touch the hilt of the sword. "My blade is bless'ed for defense, but not revenge. My heart beats hesitant. 'Tis a feeling most curious."

"The waiting does it." Symptomatic Nerve Gas is surely remembering nights along the main line of resistance in Korea. He must remember Chinese catcalls before an attack. He must remember Chinese overrunning barbed wire, mines, and machine guns; how Chinese defeated barbed wire by the simple tactic of covering it with dead men. "Have you missed anything?" he asks me. "Do we have a fall-back position in case this screws up?"

"Maybe half of a plan, but this is a well-laid hustle. Nothing should go wrong." Still, Symptomatic Nerve Gas is correct. "Always check the exits," I tell him. "When a hustle goes sour it pays to disappear." I do not tell him what else I have in mind, mostly because I can't believe it myself. I don't want to go before another camera, don't want to step back into the blare of hype. I'll do it, though, if necessary.

Silk eases backward, away from the vestibule and toward the interior of the church. She has remained troubled but calm. She looks into darkness of The Sanctuary where candles flicker. "I have lost two homes in my life," she whispers. "I will not lose another. I will not leave, not even for a minute." She points toward the

Ramirez house, now small and dark beneath its grief. "Will you ask me to abandon them in their need, just to save my skin?"

Silk, who once allowed herself to love small things only, replaces Elgin as the center of love in this place. And where does Elgin wander?

Hal stands framed in fog and pink light as he keeps watch on the street. "We'll not go from hence, my lady. I here vow." Hal's voice is slow and quiet, and I suddenly recall he is a Virginian. When southern voices are this quiet, you could not move them with explosives.

I exchange glances with Symptomatic Nerve Gas. He responds to Hal's voice. He must have known Southerners while in the Army. He shakes his head and squares his shoulders. "I'll stand right here beside you," he tells Hal. "And I'll be packing a ball bat." To me he says, "This had better work. There ain't no exits."

XX

Ezekiel 12:22: "The days are prolonged, and every vision faileth."
I stand in disbelief before a seedy drugstore, where, for the right
price, they let you write your own prescriptions. Across the street,
men with eyebrows like knuckles enter an Italian restaurant that
sports a bookie. Our hustle is going bust. Our killer is not supposed
to be this slick.

When morning arrived I called the police. I told them the stolen Jag would pass this intersection. A squad car with two cops
parked and waited. This hustle looked perfect, and now it falls
apart.

Our killer knows how to handle cops. He stepped from that car
keeping his hands in sight, walked to the front of the patrol car and
waited. Slow and easy, without a care. Our killer actually smiled.

Now he stands chewing the fat with the older cop, while the
younger cop talks on the squad car radio. In ten minutes the police
computer will clear his license and registration. I wait, hoping for a
miracle. Our killer's survival instincts are superb. You'd think he
had nothing to do all day except exchange pleasantries with police.

A pretty girl passes. The older cop allows his glance to follow her. Our murderer checks his watch. He's acting a little iffy, but maintaining control. The younger cop sits in the car and yawns. Our killer says something mildly funny. The older cop chuckles, then looks for other pretty girls.

The younger cop climbs from the car, walks to our murderer, and hands back license and registration. Our murderer says something humorous, because the older cop laughs. He actually taps our murderer on the shoulder in sign of good fellowship. The murderer climbs back in the Jag and pulls into traffic.

I'm a dollar short and a day late, but understand the mistake. This setup allowed the killer to get a good night's sleep. In my urgency to keep him off the street I allowed him rest. Had he been kept under tension this hustle would have been a wrap.

He will be under splendid tension in about fifteen minutes. It will take that long to drive to the phony address of Purity Productions. What he'll find is a dentist's office. He'll either catch on quick, or spend another fifteen minutes searching for Purity. Once he understands that he's been had, he'll start breathing fire. He will not come after us in daylight.

The killer should return home in a little over an hour. My spirit fills with desolation, but that is a luxury. I mourn the busted scam for exactly two minutes, then shrug it off. It's not a total failure. It's taken a little heat off of Silk and Elgin. It gives our murderer warning that he has a real target out here. Me.

It's time for action. Time to turn up the pressure. First, though, time for return to The Sanctuary. I must bear the news that our plan went bust.

I walk through Jericho reviewing substitutes for the botched hustle. Mardi Gras decorations remind me that the street wakes in three days. This may turn out well. My original plan called for lights and music and Danny Kaye comedy. I had not dreamed of a crowd as big as Fat Tuesday's drunkards, but size is no problem. I return to The Sanctuary in a mood approaching optimism.

Hal stands guard. He watches the Ramirez house where Silk

helps care for the Ramirez children. Elgin has not returned. Symptomatic Nerve Gas searches for him.

"The plan almost worked," I tell Hal. I explain what happened. "I have to divert him, or he'll come here. He doesn't know who is after him, but he knows Silk and Elgin asked questions."

"Here's cause for dismay," Hal says. "What diversion?"

"I have resources. I'll run him out of state."

"So he kills elsewhere." Hal is not pleased with me, although his voice holds some sympathy. "It's not a game of quoits," he says. "You throw iron rings at pegs, while I stand guard. Already Elgin's lost."

"Symptomatic Nerve Gas will find him."

"I fear he'll not." Hal is angry, but perhaps only at the situation, and I have to grant that anger. Hal withdraws into obstinacy. He tells himself he will defend Silk and her sanctuary. He may feel that I have failed us. Can I be redeemed? Of course. Hal is just.

"Let the demon ride," Hal says. "Free and squalling let him fly. I'll overcome him here, and there's the end."

"And there's the start of it for you," I tell him. "Police do not believe in demons. They'll toss you into prison."

"I doubt me it will fall that way. 'Tis necessary to subdue, not kill. His attack speaks grounds for his arrest." Hal watches the Ramirez house. His hands hang loose, yet his posture is attentive. I know how quickly he can move, like the white spirit of wind. "You are a player," he says, "and did you ever kill 'twas on a stage. The curtain drew. Your victim rose smiling." His hands tense momentarily, then relax. "No fault attach when one kills in defense." He's talking to himself, not me. He sounds like he tries to convince himself, and darkness stands in those dark eyes.

He nearly throws me out of role. No wonder he's a remittance man. Is he wanted for murder in Virginia? He glances at me, sees my dismay.

"The sorry snapping of a neck," he tells me. "The man was loutish in his rape. His head dangled most curious. A jury found me blameless. The woman lived. Her testimony saved me."

His youth and gentleness denies the story, but Hal does not lie. I wonder if his defense of some woman in Virginia drove him into monomania. Once again I see his young idealism that has survived its first hard blows. I had not believed the blows were that hard.

"Grant me my attempt," I ask. "If I fail, the demon will still come here. I don't want you to break another neck." I pause, not believing the garbage I hear coming from my mouth. Where is my humanity? Surely Hal needs comforting, not indifference. "I want to save Silk from fear. You are very dear to her, to us."

"To stave her fear is also a man's work." Hal sees the sense of what I say, although he does not soften toward me. "It's on your head should aught happen to her." His voice is so quiet it would frighten an army.

"He'll make no move during the day. Try to get some rest."

"Anon."

Hal stands wakeful sentry as I leave. Hal may not like it, and *I* may not like it, but my first duty is to get rid of this guy. If I run him out of town, then tell the police about him, they are more likely to be interested than if he stayed in place. He may kill again, that's true. On the other hand, he's going to do it, anyway. If I can't run him out, then all of us will be attending Mardi Gras.

Words are weapons—Job 6:25: "How forcible are right words"— and a phone gives one enough distance for protection. I choose a phone booth in the lobby of what was once a swell hotel. Our killer answers on the fourth ring. The killer's voice seems only a little shaken. It is husky, and in the female role. I can imagine her long and muscular legs beneath short skirt; the distinctive nose and expensive wig. I nearly shudder thinking of those square and powerful hands. This will be interesting.

"Josie," I say in a voice both soft and strong, "this is your father. What's bothering my little girl?" I let the words hang.

A quick intake of breath. A confused stammer. Something very like a sob. There's slight choking, as if she's fighting back a scream. Her reactions tell me we've got a split personality here, because shock does not knock her out of role. That's bad news. In a very real way we're dealing with two killers, not one. She's gradually regaining control.

"I don't know who you are. Why are you doing this?" Then she pauses. ". . . you sonovabitch."

I remain silent. If her personality holds true to the usual serial murderer, she'll start to run a con. These charlatans are verbally adept.

"If this is an obscene call, at least make it interesting. I *could* be in the mood. Are you for chains and whips, or only whipped cream?" She's fishing, and fishing very well. Her voice regains poise. There's a combination of sexuality and little-girl wholesomeness. She should be anchoring the evening news. What a loss to television.

"It is about obscenity," I tell her. "Murder is obscene."

Now her voice tinkles. "That's kinky. You're going to murder me over the phone."

Silence is also a weapon. One-Timothy 2:11: "Let the woman learn in silence with all subjection." I lean against the side of the phone booth and study the problem. It's clear that the male role suffered enormous disappointment. Maybe he even suffered grief. He's not going to be on television. Instead of handling the disappointment, the male role submerged, and handed the whole emotional mess over to the woman. This, of course, is known as chickenshit. The information may be useful.

She's also waiting, giving nothing away, preparing for the next gambit. She figures we've got a Mexican standoff. She's in a game she won't win. These killers are so self-absorbed they love their own voices.

"Let's talk about you," she says. "I've heard your voice somewhere." Her voice is coy, and she's making a nice move. "Are you an older gentleman?"

"We'll get to that," I tell her. "Let's talk about the best way for you to turn yourself in to the police. I advise a lawyer."

Silence. She must be covering the phone with her hand while

she's catching her breath. When she regains control her voice is cool. "If you're a cop, you're blowing smoke. You know the rules of entrapment. You know about harassment."

I can't let her get too angry. If she gets too angry she'll hang up. I couldn't call back, because that would display a weak hand. "I am not the police," I say gently, "and there's no phone tap. You've got a problem, Josie." I can't believe the amount of love sounding in my voice. I'm talking to a beast that has killed more than forty women, and yet I speak to the small amount of humanity that might still remain in her head. "You've been running scared for a long time, kid."

She thinks she's got an edge. She figures she's talking to a preacher, or to someone from the Mission. I didn't mean to con her, but she's conned. A good thing, too, because the situation was about to get out of hand. When she comes back on she's running her own scam. She begins a rap about needing spiritual advice. She admits she's lonely. She infers that she loves the Lord, but has lost her way.

These serial killers are adept, but not very bright. Half of their success depends on being dumb enough to feel invincible. It took several years to catch Ted Bundy, not because he was smart, but because he was mediocre.

"We could meet somewhere," she says. "You can help me. Maybe come to my house."

It's time to bring her back down. I keep my voice calm, but now it carries a bit of chill. "I've been to your house. You have photographs of yourself on the walls." I describe the photographs. "You leave your knives on the dressing table." I describe the knives. There's a lot of silence on the other end. Out there in the street a police siren squalls. I hold the phone away from my ear and toward the sound. Maybe she hears it.

This creature has violated the bodies and lives of women, and now it is feeling violated. Someone has apparently been inside its house. There's a certain amount of pleasure in this, but I do not let it show.

She replies in a voice that tries to control its fright. She's not acting. A man would be enraged, but Josie is not a man. She's a woman who has been ravished in no small way. "Don't do this," she says. "Don't do any more of this."

"My feelings exactly," I tell her. "You must do no more of what you're doing. Stop killing. Go to the police. Get help."

Silence breaks before muffled sobs. Then her voice sounds nearly relieved. "My brother just came home," she says. "Just a minute. Talk to my brother."

Here's a twist, and I care nothing at all for it. I stand listening to silence while knowing what is happening. She's passing the personality over to her brother.

This is nearly as rare as the Loch Ness monster. Most split personalities cannot be passed. They only change when one or the other becomes ascendant. I know of only one documented case of voluntary passing of personality. It will be interesting to see if they can pull this off.

They pull it off very well. When *he* comes on, I'm talking to a man. He's a completely different person. I'd be shocked, if, in my wanderings, I had not encountered split personalities. The first time you run into it, you can't believe it's happening.

"You made Josie cry," he says in a quiet voice. "I'll not forget that. Cut the jive. Get on with it." He sounds businesslike, the way he must sound when passing one of his sleazy real estate deals. "You're trying a shakedown. How much?"

"It isn't that easy," I tell him. "You'll either turn yourself in, or get dragged in. I'm your nemesis, pal."

He's silent, but there's nothing defensive about it. I can feel him thinking of the best way to attack. I wonder if he's feeling silly, standing by the phone in Josie's dress and wig. Maybe he's taken the wig off.

"How was your television spot?" I ask. "It's a great career move." I speak quietly. It's necessary to rattle him, but if we get to yelling there's room for mistakes.

He's angry, but holding it. "I don't know who you are. I know about a woman with a big mouth, and about a scrawny little nigger.

Losers. Why deal with some bum who has a quarter for a phone call?"

"You're a killer," I say quietly. "There isn't a place far enough, or a hole deep enough, for you to hide. Tuck it in, bud. It's over."

"If you had anything to say we wouldn't be talking. All you've got is bullshit. Call a cop." It's a nice bluff, and I have to admire the way he's handling this. He hasn't the foggiest notion who I am. Time to turn up the heat.

"I have pictures." My lie sounds truthful. "Telephoto lens." I change to my TV producer's voice. "Don't underestimate your opposition." I change to my MBA businesswoman's voice. "You deal with forces beyond your market." I switch to my secretarial voice. "If you underestimate me, your phone will catch fire and your dick will fall off." I say this sweetly. Then I shift to Josie's voice. "This is getting serious."

I've finally got the bastard's attention. He chokes. "Josie has nothing to do with anything. Who in the hell are you."

I've got him hooked, and about ready to run. "You pose an interesting judicial problem," I tell him. "If you plead guilty to murder, and exonerate Josie, the court can't sentence her. You'd get a free pass. At worst you'd get a few years in a nut ward. I'd give it a try, pal. You'll make TV." I'm hitting a little hard, but this is working well and he can stand it. He may actually be fond of his sister. As perverse as this gent is, they may be lovers.

He's actually thinking about it. He's wondering if Josie can stand up under interrogation. These split personalities often have fair knowledge of each other. It would be the biggest media event since Watergate. He's seeing himself as principal actor, seeing Josie as helpless victim receiving sympathy from the court.

Now he stops thinking about it, even though, for him, it may be an acceptable fantasy. Plus, Josie is also a murderer.

He's fishing. "There's a thousand guys out there who could be guilty."

"There's a thousand guys out here who *are* guilty," I tell him, "but, pal, you're wholesaling." I let him sit with that for ten seconds, largely because he's too cool. He's getting to me. Then I come back at him in a deranged voice. It is not hard to do because I'm remembering Teeney and Maria. I'm thinking that Katie is being set up to be murdered. This is not supposed to be happening. I was supposed to make him angry, but he's turned it around and I'm suddenly furious. "You have a wee problem," I tell him, "because I'm as crazy as you are. Maybe crazier." I let go of a deranged laugh, and it goes on longer than expected. This almost isn't theater. "I have as many faces as I have voices," I tell him. "You'll want to think about that."

"You've only got one asshole," he says. "And it can be reamed . . . if you want to talk about knives."

The voice on the phone changes. Something is happening here, and it's all different. There's complete disregard for safety in this voice. The tones are higher, and they hiss. Is this a third personality, something demonic?

"Or," the voice hisses, "if you're a woman you've got two tits. Funny stuff can happen to tits."

"I owe you two of something," I tell him, but now he has me shaking. I don't know what this guy is—what this *thing* is. "Do you remember a nice lady who followed you to the public market? Do you remember an old gentleman who you chased into a department store? You *killed* my roles." My voice is higher than I want, more vulnerable.

I've made a mistake, or maybe it isn't. Now he figures he deals with a looney. This whole show depends on convincing him I'm a dangerous looney.

"Chill out, man." He actually chuckles, but it's like one of the voices that live in the belltower of The Sanctuary. "You're good, but are you that good?" He digs for information, trying to take a sight on my true identity. Lots of luck, buddy. Right now I don't even know if I have one.

I grab a couple of deep breaths. "You're done." I've got my voice under nice control. It's a relief, but he's knocked me out of role. "How does it feel to have to look over your shoulder all the time, the way women have to look over their shoulders. How does it feel to be hunted?"

"It feels okay, and I'll tell you what will happen. I'll dress what's left of you in a black nightie." He sure isn't thinking hard enough. This cat operates on store-bought fantasies, not imagination.

"You've got three options." This time my voice is cold as vengeance. "You can kill yourself. You can turn yourself in. You can get out of town, in which case it will take the cops a little longer."

He starts to speak, maybe to say he's got four choices. Then he can't help himself, he's forced to elaborate. "You are pork chops, man. Pieces of you on a plate."

This is getting out of hand. I try to push him harder, but he's got the edge. "No matter where you go, I may be there," I tell him. "I may be a woman who sells real estate. I may be the guy in the sports car next to you in traffic. I may be the rent-a-cop at your bank. I'm baker and candlestick maker; and you're the butcher." This bastard deals in terrorism. Let him see how it feels. "If you leave your house, I may be sitting there with cops, waiting for you when you come home."

"It slices both ways." He's almost giggling, still trying to push me to more revelations. I've already said too much.

"It all depends on who gets the first slice," I tell him. "The only safe place for you is a police station. You've got seventy-two hours. In seventy-two hours, you become a media event. Your ugly face goes on camera. I'm planning a big show, nothing quiet."

"We'll meet. Count on it."

"We meet in front of a camera. If you're not gone in seventy-two hours you're history. If you can't think straight for yourself, then think of Josie."

163

I hang up with a sense of failure. It is time to shelve this role. This role already has the next move figured, and this role is dangerous. It's too easy to slide out, and I nearly fudged my shot.

There was too much real madness in my voice, but no depth of insanity matches what I heard in his. I feel the role flickering away in a diminishing echo. Proverbs 26:13: "... there *is* a lion in the way; a lion *is* in the streets."

ACT
FIVE

XXI

Silken Silk, silky she glides, approaching past the Soft Porn Grocery, tall and nearly sinuous in gray wool suit discarded by some perfumed lady. Silk's feet touch the ground, but do not seem to, as she returns to her sanctuary. She steps confident beside those colorful swirls of demented energy; graffiti staking out gang turf.

I wait beside Hal and Symptomatic Nerve Gas. My next moves are evident to me, but not to them. They are on defense, and even I have a sense of urgency. At the same times it's best to wait for the murderer's next move. My own show does not open until Mardi Gras.

Silence lives in the belltower. Even demons hesitate. The game is in desperate and delicate balance.

"She's looking perky." Symptomatic Nerve Gas sounds hopeful. "It's about time something good happened."

Hal stands in silent misery. Word on the street says that two neighborhood children were molested in a nearby park. They are alive, but hysterical. Hal was not there to save them. He stood guard at The Sanctuary. Hal blames himself for not being in two places at the same time.

It is Friday afternoon, getting along toward evening. Next Tuesday is Mardi Gras. Much of what I do depends on the murderer. Will he run, or hide, or attack? I told him he had seventy-two hours. He must make his move by Monday evening.

On the other side of the street Van Loon steps from his house and looks into the lowering gloom. Katie Van Loon has not returned from school. Already she is two hours late. Van Loon stands squarish as a blond brick, but his face is emotional. He looks toward The Sanctuary. To a stolid Dutch burgher we must look freakish. Frustration and anger override Van Loon's methodical ways. I pity the man who crosses him.

Katie is nowhere in sight. Van Loon stands with hands in jacket pockets, and in one of those pockets there no doubt nestles a pistol. If our murderer could see Van Loon, would our murderer shudder or feel victorious? All of those murdered girls had fathers. I momentarily imagine more than forty fathers walking the streets with pistols. It would cause a bloodbath of a kind only Hal would accept. Hal is a defender, but Virginians of his stamp understand revenge.

Weather is chill but not cold. Steps of The Sanctuary are nearly dry. The three of us sit, and Hal spreads a jacket for Silk. We have not sat outside and watched the street for a long, long time. Soon the pink poodle above the homosexual bar will ignite like a silly sunrise. There's lots of hustle and bustle going on as the joint adds many decorations. Mardi Gras is the biggest day and night of the year at the homosexual bar. There's always quite a show.

"Elgin is safe." Silk says this while halfway up the steps. "He's staying at the apartment of a real old woman. He's not talking much to anyone, except to Jorge Ramirez." She takes a seat beside Hal. Her happiness does much to dispel Hal's gloom.

"His scrawny little butt belongs here where he's safe." Symptomatic Nerve Gas has his feelings hurt. For my own part, I can't blame Elgin if he seeks safety elsewhere.

"And why is he messing around with Ramirez? Ramirez is a

cupcake." Symptomatic Nerve Gas watches, as, across the street, Van Loon turns back to reenter his house. Vandermeer's Great Dane woofs. There are no songs or giggles of children. No one plays hopscotch before the truck axle company.

"Ramirez suffers wounds most grievous," Hal says. "We may not take him lightly. There's thunder in the offing."

"Elgin asked me if I could ruin that black van. He'd ought to say if he wants it taken out."

We know that Symptomatic Nerve Gas has an old Buick station wagon parked out back. We know he has made preparations, but we do not know what he plans. All we really know is that our man has seen too much death. Symptomatic Nerve Gas will not kill our murderer, but I would not give short odds on the survival of that van.

"I am not afraid," Silk says. "At least I'm not afraid for myself. Elgin is a powerful man. Maybe I'm afraid of such power." She sits beside Hal, and her understanding of power is greater than mine. I don't know what she's talking about. Silk sits, ignorant of my love. I've been scrupulous in keeping it from her. Belov'ed Silk, child of grace, how may this poor actor serve?

The poodle sign flashes on. Pink light floods the darkening street. Commuter traffic moves jerkily, and across roofs of cars dance little tailings of pink. Parked autos are like hibernating beasts.

A tall shadow emerges from the Soft Porn Grocery. The man wears a down jacket and sock hat. He hits the bricks running. It appears the Soft Porn has been robbed again. The man disappears down an alley. No one else emerges from the Soft Porn. I assume they are all dead over there, or, more likely, sensibly hiding. Hal stands, stretches, sits back down. He will not leave his post. Symptomatic Nerve Gas pops his knuckles and seems trying to make up his mind. "Hang tight," he says to Hal. "I'll see if they need help." Symptomatic Nerve Gas moves away at a steady but unhurried pace. He knows how long it takes to die from wounds. Whatever has happened is already over.

Silk rises to follow. Hal touches her elbow, motions her to sit. "Had there been shots I would have kenned. Mayhap this spells deception."

Commuter traffic continues, but no one walks out there. When trouble flares, street-smart people disappear. Symptomatic Nerve Gas is a lone figure who hesitates before passing the mouth of the alley. He peers into darkness, assures himself no one is there, and continues toward the Soft Porn. He enters the store, then exits in twenty seconds. We have to guess that nothing has happened. We guess this really is some sort of deception.

A lone figure approaches from half a block away. She walks with the swing of a young girl. Pink light floods the sidewalk, and, as she steps into the light, we see Katie Van Loon. She carries a shopping bag. With his back to the alley, Symptomatic Nerve Gas stands watching her.

From the mouth of the alley the black van eases forward like a huge insect. Silk gasps. Hal moves, spontaneous as wind. I shout, but my voice drowns beneath the clang of traffic. The van sits like a dark monument to evil, and pink light glosses the faces of painted demons. An interior light glows as our murderer opens the door. Our murderer is quick, and he moves toward Symptomatic Nerve Gas. I shout again, but the only voices rising above traffic come from the belltower.

And then it is all over. Katie Van Loon sees the van. She half runs, half skips toward it, and she makes clumsy waves with the shopping bag. The murderer sees her, dives back into the van, and pulls into traffic. He swings the wheel hard, taking the van across two lanes as horns blare and brakes squall. Hal stands watching and helpless. Everyone is still alive. Disappointed voices mutter in the belltower.

"Saved by a kid." Symptomatic Nerve Gas is embarrassed. He forgot to protect his back. We sit on the steps of The Sanctuary as commuter traffic eases. Silk still trembles, and so do I. Hal is far too silent. His temper rises like the controlled heat of a blast furnace.

Katie Van Loon has entered her house, but not before she hid the shopping bag beneath the front step. Van Loon will be raising hell over there. He no doubt yells when he should be listening.

"I didn't think the murderer would be this bold," I say to Symptomatic Nerve Gas. "And now he's seen both you and Hal." Of all of us, I'm the only one who is still partly invisible. The murderer has only seen my roles.

"He'll be back." Symptomatic Nerve Gas watches the street, and, by Heaven, he's correct. The guy is going around. The black van rises in traffic. It nearly loafs past The Sanctuary. Is the murderer laughing at us? On his third time around he actually parks in a bus stop. The van sits not fifty yards off in a pool of pink light. When Hal moves, the van drives away.

"This ain't getting it. I'm going to take him out." Symptomatic Nerve Gas is so positive, his voice so harsh, that I wonder if we're wrong. Maybe he really will kill. He turns to me. "I want you to go through this place. Check every door and window. Make sure we're boarded up." He turns to Silk. "Hold a flashlight for me. I've got a half hour's tinkering." He starts down the steps, headed around the building to the parked station wagon. Then he pauses with an afterthought. "Bring some rags," he tells Silk. "We'll wipe it clean of prints. I registered the damn thing in the name of the mayor."

The basement of this old church resembles catacombs. I carry a kerosene lamp through empty and forgotten rooms. Lamplight plays along a main corridor, low-ceilinged, small rooms on one side and the building's foundation on the other. No one ever comes here, and perhaps we avoid this place because we do not wish to see the glisten of groundwater working its way through stone foundations. The basement is large for a building constructed at the turn of the century. I imagine primitive and steam-powered equipment, explosives to blast rock, a hundred men with shovels. The builders foundationed in rock, then laid brick upon the rock. Craftsmanship stands all around in precisely fitted stone. Ground-

171

water turns everything musty. Stench of lime from concrete and whitewash has turned to a flavorless smell.

There is one large room down here that may have been used for Sunday School or women's meetings. It has a boarded door that leads to stairs. The stairs ascend to the street. A steel grate on the sidewalk now covers this old entry. An intruder would have to lift the grate, then batter down the door. I haul at the boards with all my weight. There is slight give, and the boards are wet. Basement windows are boarded, but anyone could kick them in. We are vulnerable.

Lamplight reveals moldy furnishings deemed useless when this place was abandoned. There are extra pews, broken chairs, a flimsy lectern covered with moisture and decay.

I can trust Symptomatic Nerve Gas to do his best. At the same time I must do my best. I have a role saved back that guarantees complete invisibility, but I'll not use it yet. Instead of role, I will use disguise. Disguises will allow me to move around with considerable freedom. Our murderer does not capitulate. It is time to turn up the pressure.

I climb stairs to ground level. A back door to The Sanctuary stands heavily boarded. There is no give in the boards, and up here the nails are not rusty. Stained-glass windows are easily broken, and some *are* broken; but none offer space large enough for a man to climb through.

When I return to the front steps Hal and Silk stand wordless. The station wagon parks just beyond the bus stop. The tailgate hangs like a tongue. Symptomatic Nerve Gas is nowhere in sight.

"He has a little electric gidget," Silk tells me. "He's hiding down there between two cars, waiting for the van to pull into the bus stop." Her voice trembles. "I think there's going to be an explosion."

Do we trust him or not? I sit on the steps waiting for the van to appear. Has Symptomatic Nerve Gas slipped over the line and turned into a killer? If he does this thing, and the rest of us stand silent, are we not also guilty?

On the other hand, it seems we must trust him. He is not going to be dissuaded. He promised Elgin he would stop the van, but hurt no one inside. Nothing I have tried has worked.

I sit on the steps as night turns into a long and weary watch. After midnight, traffic becomes sporadic. At two A.M. the poodle sign on the homosexual bar winks out. The street remains deserted. The van does not appear.

Hal has nothing to say. I fancy he suffers both anger and grief. Silk watches with us for hours, then goes to her bed. When first dawn appears between ragged clouds I head for the sacristy and sleep. The murderer has not come back, but Symptomatic Nerve Gas has not moved that station wagon, either.

XXII

Sleep's sweet benison ceases by noon Saturday, and I wake to the day's tasks. It is clear we are to become creatures of the night for awhile. There's little fear of a daylight attack. I prepare quickly, but carefully. My disguise is a forty-year-old householder having trouble with his car. I have a receding hairline, and wear clothes that were once good, but are now worn to grubbies. I have a bandage over one knuckle where a wrench slipped, and carry a small crescent wrench in my back pocket. It will be necessary to visit that old station wagon. I need dark rings of grease beneath my fingernails, and a smudge of grease high on one cheek. If I run into any problems I'll put on the desperate look of a man in need of a rebuilt fuel pump for a '71 Fiat.

Silk has pulled a chair to the vestibule of The Sanctuary. She watches the street. Hal lies beside her, curled and asleep in his buffalo robe. Just inside the church Symptomatic Nerve Gas snores as he lies on my arctic sleeping bag. He covers himself with an old army blanket.

"Elgin is with the Ramirez family," Silk whispers. "There's five or six women sewing. I don't know what they're making. Ramirez went off to work."

"I will return before dark," I tell her. The parking space before the bus stop stands empty. "Where's the station wagon?"

"He moved it around back. He'll bring it out again after dark." Silk's delicate face holds such uncertainty. At the same time she looks at me with affection, maybe love. If love, there's unfortunately nothing needful about it. I depart, and I'm headed out to spy on Jericho.

Cars are ugly things, but when they get enough dents and rust above bald tires they gain a kind of dignity. There's no problem finding grease. Symptomatic Nerve Gas has a contrivance lumped together in the rear of the wagon, covered with old rags. The car sits in complete safety. It is such a wreck not even a drugger would raid it.

The bus ride to the north end is uneventful. Mixed clouds bring spatters of rain and spatters of sun, occasionally at the same time. Gutters carry little water. The street is nearly dry. Street trees are not yet in leaf, but buds begin to swell. Spring brings life according to poets, new car loans according to bankers. A time of renewal. The season itself says this murderer is about to become past tense. He deals only in death.

I leave the bus and begin walking. When I come to a corner from which I can spy the murderer's house I dawdle. This is a quick errand, but it pays to see all parts:

Folks, we seem to have a winner.

A mover's truck stands in the murderer's driveway. The XK-140 is nowhere seen. The black van is gone. Two kids carry packing material into the house, while the driver drops the tailgate, removing hand truck and piano board. The truck is a North Carolina–style licensed for intrastate only. That means the murderer sends his stuff to storage. He's not taking it with him. He won't towbar a Jag, so one vehicle must be stashed in somebody's storage lot.

I return to the bus stop with mixed feelings of fatalism and anger. The bum may be leaving town, but you can bet he isn't going to stop killing. I've sentenced other young girls on some other street. At the same time, there was no choice except to make him run.

And, the game is not over. Whether he's still in town or not, we'll bring this tootsie down come Tuesday night.

I take the disguise of an honest man. No costume is necessary; it's a matter of attitude, and I head for the homosexual bar. When I enter, the place stands silent; although bustle-noises from the back show that someone prepares for this night's activities.

The owner of this bar is a queen of the old school. I knew him in days when he was a hack for an ad agency. There's respect in my head, and no small amount of love in my heart for this guy. He remembers a youth filled with scorn and occasional beatings. He met his dates in bad places; public restrooms, flea-bait motels, and abandoned basements. He hid his practices from family and friends. He dodged police, and got his pumpkin head busted with night-sticks when he did not dodge fast enough. No one can think he's a pansy. He lived through deadly times, but times have changed. In some ways being a homosexual is now a mark of excellence.

When he comes from the back room he carries three flats of canned beer. He's tall and skinny like a cowboy, but with silver hair that is not just styled, it's manicured. He wears a chambray work shirt over his fancily stitched western shirt. It looks like the bar's theme for tonight will be the Wild, Wild West.

"Where in hell have you been? It's amazing what a guy runs into when he's not carrying his gun." He seems pleased to see me.

I'm not about to tell him that I live over at The Sanctuary. For one thing, he wouldn't believe it.

"You look like a Spanish don is a cowboy suit," I say. "Jim, it's good to see you."

"What's your hustle?" He checks his watch. "Wine cooler," he says absentmindedly. "We open up directly." He looks past me, checking bottles in a standup refrigeration case.

"Street theater for Mardi Gras," I tell him. "I want to set up on your sidewalk. I need to wire lights from your building."

He's interested, largely because he knows I'm a pro. "Tell me," he says.

Time begins to dance. As we become watchful creatures of the night, time slows, then speeds, then slows again. Time measures itself by the flow of the street, not by the flow of hours. Saturday night opens with short skirts and low-cut blouses, with coke-happy hookers, with Cad pimp-mobiles, and singing bells from a far-off church. Television glows from darkened houses of Van Loon, Vandermeer, Ramirez. As night deepens the homosexual bar hosts cowboys and cowgirls and Indians, easy costumes on a routine Saturday night. The big show comes next Tuesday.

We hammer nails as we put more boards across windows. The neighborhood seems on defense. Elgin is with Ramirez. Katie Van Loon remains at home in sulkish misery. Symptomatic Nerve Gas parks the Buick. He waits, and waits—and waits.

Our murderer has not left town. Why has he sent his belongings to storage? It must mean that he intends to leave, after some last act. I do not understand his game, only know that fear and anger drive him. By now he may have discovered me, may know the identity of everyone who lives here. The black van rises behind the cars of johns and pimps. It goes around, then goes around again. It does not park, and then it disappears.

Night snuggles toward silence as the street begins to empty. A pink pall lies across sidewalks, and light mist hovers over Jericho.

Sunday begins good, ends fearful. Sunday sees me on the phone. I know every actor in this city, and ninety percent of them look for work. Since this will be street theater I want actors who are Hell's Angels of the intellect. I need actors who have souls of buccaneers, the moxie of killer-angels. We need quick minds and quick mouths. "Improv," I tell them. "About all you get is costume, set, and situation. I want the kind of jive that San Francisco Mime came with, back when they were good."

I plan a courtroom scene. Television cameras will cover the stage. As the trial moves along, there will come a time when witnesses are called. I will go to the stage as a witness, and give my greatest performance. When I identify the murderer—and when my act hits a half million TV screens—the police will be forced to uncover every move the demon has ever made.

I return to The Sanctuary and a funerary basket of flowers awaits to club me with fear; tall lilies, severe black bow, stiff ferns. A card of condolence mentions my name. Symptomatic Nerve Gas watches me for signs of fear. Hal stands beside me as protector. He does not understand the full import of the flowers—nor do I—but gentle Hal defends. "A mawkish trick by a poor trickster," Hal says.

"A young man in a flower truck delivered them," Silk tells me. "Just a delivery boy. He only did as he was told." She touches my forearm with her fingertips, but the touch is only sisterly. She waits for me to explain the meaning of these flowers.

Fear tries to bring forth a shriek, and I fear not the murderer, but the flowers. It takes a short spell before I'm breathing normally.

"He's better than I thought," I admit to Silk. "At least we know how he's spent his days."

Our murderer has made his living by researching forgotten plots of real estate. He's an expert researcher. Now he's researched until he's discovered me. It was not an easy trail, but anyone with skill could have followed it. "He's still a fool," I tell Silk. "He's let us know that he'll attack. All this does is define the game." I wish I felt as confident as I sound. This killer is elaborate.

"You can always count on a smart-ass to make mistakes." Symptomatic Nerve Gas leaves us to move the station wagon into its parking place. I do not know if he speaks about the murderer, or about me.

Sunday night brings voices from the belltower. The black van cruises, goes around three times, and does not park. Hal is getting feisty. Silk soothes him. Time dances, flows, speeds up, then slows. Symptomatic Nerve Gas waits.

Monday is my busy day. No good can come from hiding. The game is wide open and must be played. The murderer will follow my every move. My last defense is a role that he will not be able to penetrate. I rent a portable stage, portable lights, and costumes. Since this will be street theater it must be illicit. We can't get permits. If we are legal we will offend the spirit of our play. The sectioned stage and portable lights get stashed at the homosexual bar.

While this happens I call the biggest duckie in local television. She is a greatly loved flack with the evening news, and she knows me well enough to understand she's got a story. "We will unmask the murderer," I tell her. "It's a rerun of Hamlet, whereby we trap the conscience . . . and the walls come tumblin'." My metaphor is mixed, but she doesn't know it. All she knows is that she's about to hatch the year's biggest story. "You've got it exclusive," I tell her, "as long as you *do* it. Otherwise, it goes to Channel 4." I hang up happy as a teddy bear in kindergarten.

Monday night finds us watchful. I gave the murderer seventy-two hours. We figure something is about to happen. The street seems paused before possibility. A French frigate makes a visit to this city's docks. French sailors stroll and whores are jubilant. The Frenchies make colorful contrast to shopworn johns and pimps. At Cathedral Mansion a cracked-out biker yells that foreigners are fucking American girls, but he soon loses interest in protectionism. Traffic cruises Monday-night-light. A lot of dear folk still nurse hangovers from the weekend. The homosexual bar does little business. Pink neon glows above deserted sidewalks. Hal and Silk and I sit on the steps of The Sanctuary. Drizzle will soon drive us to cover. Elgin is with Ramirez. Symptomatic Nerve Gas crouches between cars. He still hopes to trap the black van, and from the belltower comes enough racket for me to believe he will. To paraphrase a leading expert: What's born of fire belongs to fire, and so I fear Hell's certain.

I sit on the front steps and watch the street while mentally preparing my new role. I will be a black forty-three-year-old street musician. As a younger man I played jazz, but the viciousness of the music industry finally drove me to the street. In early days on the street I tried every form of music in an attempt to make coins fall into my trumpet case. I played sweet, and I played hot. I played classical, and, during one awful season, I tried country. Nothing worked.

Then I struck the magic combination. In complete disgust I began to blat. It started as sarcasm; tunes in middle range, overattacks on every note; blatting hard enough to crack notes—and the coins began to drop. The worse I played the more I made. On the Fourth of July I played Christmas carols. I studied to become obnoxious. I now dress in raggedy clothing. Instead of a trumpet case for collecting coins, I use a plastic bucket. I tried different nasty signs on the bucket. Final breakthrough came when I lettered a sign reading "No Canadian Coins." On a good day I knock down twenty dollars an hour.

These days I hit the bricks only on weekends, or on festive occasions. During the week, when night arrives, I climb to the top of a hill in this city's arboretum, and play jazz into the wind. Or, I stand on a deserted pier and blow Bach chorales across the waves of Puget Sound.

The ghosts of Teeney and Maria walk this Monday night. They are pale spirits who drift through pink drizzle and pink mist. No doubt the spirits of more than forty girls float beside the halting English and liquid French of sailors. Teeney was such a little girl. Maria was chubby and happy.

And, no doubt, their murderer is out here as well. Even now he may—or she may—be conning some young woman. They speak of pantyhose, of costume jewelry, of stylish breeds of dogs. They discuss designer croissants, or lace underwear. Our murderer is the ultimate consumer.

Darkest horror threatens to wrap around me. The sin is mine. I've used my sacred craft to make slick commercials. I've ridden the tamed horse of trade, and what came from it is lots of money, plus this deep horror. The murderer is at least partly my creature.

"The night is out of kilter." Silk looks not at the street, but to the black interior of The Sanctuary where a few candle flames dance like golden spirits. They illuminate the red of stained-glass windows, but all else is dark as medieval night.

" 'Tis demons with their sulfur breath," Hal says. "They ride the darkness as in olden days."

I can't argue with him. There are mutters in the belltower. Silk turns back to the street. She is startled.

The black van slows, seems about to park, then continues slowly. The murderer reconnoiters. He can see us here on the steps.

"Stand by. Take a strain. I think our fish is in the net." I stand and pretend to be confused. I exaggerate uncertainty, trying to ease the murderer's fears. It's time to reel this sucker in.

At the end of the block he hangs a right. He's going around. Symptomatic Nerve Gas is a dark form hunkered between two cars. He doubtless sees what happens. He waits motionless.

The black van rises in light traffic. It seems even larger, somehow, more ominous. Pink light does not soften painted flames surrounding painted demons. The van slows, then slides into the bus stop behind the station wagon, braking easily, headlights off and parking lights agleam; and, from the darkness between cars, rising like the clash of arms, comes the command voice of Symptomatic Nerve Gas. "Gotcha, bastard, I finally *gotcha.*"

A small sun lights in the back of the station wagon and a flow of liquid sun seems to roll almost slowly in an expanding wave. As it rolls it builds, glass shattering from side windows of the wagon, glass dancing red and pink across the wet street. I do not know how

Symptomatic Nerve Gas manages this, but it is a controlled explosion; fire surging in a constantly increasing wave; fire embracing the front of the black van as demon faces light with fire. Fire gushes like a river as windshields crack with sudden heat—as painted demons grow black, as gray and black smoke rise from burning tires—while fire expands. Fire searches beneath the van, spreads sideways into the street. There is movement behind those windshields. The murderer reacts quickly, if you consider his shock, and firelight shows his form twisting away from the driver's seat as he heads for the rear of the van. The liquid sun of fire continues to pour, and, in the midst of it, comes a loud thump as the gas tank of the station wagon explodes. Traffic stops, is blocked, cars honk and fenders clash as the nearest automobiles try to back away. Grease and oil beneath the van catch fire, and the van sits like a dragon bathed in its own flame. A nance comes from the homosexual bar, turns back and yells. A small group of happy, swishy people gather beneath pink neon and cheer. Hoots and whoops come from bikers at Cathedral Mansion. Steam rises through flame as the radiator hoses crumple. The van is now approaching meltdown.

From behind parked cars Symptomatic Nerve Gas moves with quickness learned from combat, but he carries no rifle, only a ball bat. Hal's shadow flies toward the van, and Hal's blond hair makes him a whitely moving spirit through darkness and flame. Silk and I follow, but our pace is slow compared to our friends.

Fire rises along the sides of the van, while the station wagon sits like a coffin of fire. A joking French voice rises about the roar of flame and clank of traffic. It speaks gutter French to a shipmate, and translates roughly as: "Americans are such showoffs." The back doors of the van swing wide as Symptomatic Nerve Gas arrives. A dark figure leaps into the street, stumbles, falls and rolls. It regains its feet as Symptomatic Nerve Gas nails it with an open field tackle. The two figures roll, then Symptomatic Nerve Gas stands. He seems confused. The other figure flees. It is small, chunky, but runs on light feet like the skittering of a frightened spirit. Symptomatic Nerve Gas picks up his ball bat, then turns to catch Hal's arm as

Hal passes, chasing the fleeing demon. Both men are strong, but Hal is young.

"It was a kid. A young girl. Just a *kid*. We're conned."

Hal tugs away, then hears. He pauses.

"Put your butts in reverse. That thing is going to blow." Symptomatic Nerve Gas pushes me, Silk, and Hal. "We'll have cops in two minutes."

By the time the van explodes we stand before the steps of The Sanctuary. The explosion comes from a full gas tank, and does not simply thump. It lifts the rear of the van, spreading fire across pavement so that the stench of cooking asphalt is layered through drizzling rain. Bikers cheer, sailors hoot, and homosexuals giggle. Doorways of houses open. Figures stand in the doorways, watching the fire. Vandermeer, Van Loon, Ramirez.

Katie Van Loon ducks beneath her father's arm and runs toward the street. She stands watching the van, and then she screams, and screams; cannot seem to stop screaming. Silk walks toward her, wanting to give solace, but Van Loon pulls Katie away. He brings her back to the house, but one more scream rises in the night before the door swings closed. Police sirens approach. When they are no more than a block away the street empties. No one has seen anything.

"What the hell was all that about?" Symptomatic Nerve Gas has performed dangerously, but with a certain amount of good taste when we consider that we oppose a demon. "That kid may have been driving that van around for three nights."

"The murderer bought time by having a young girl drive," I say. "He wanted us to think he remained in town, so he conned one of the street kids into driving. It must have been fun for her. Meanwhile, our murderer heads out. He could be nearly to the east coast by now." I can think of no other reason for the deception. I have to admire the way he worked his hustle, have to admire the planning. Our murderer could have sent flowers to me from anywhere. I do not understand how he discovered my identity so quickly, not if he

183

left town two or three days ago. This could be a trick, or could it? I see no other explanation.

We watch as firemen douse dwindling flames, and cops unsnarl traffic. The station wagon and the van are two burned boxes. They no longer even resemble vehicles. Steel sags, and the hulks are rust colored beneath pink light. A lot of happy hooting comes from the belltower. I feel deflated in this aftermath. Our murderer is gone. That may not affect our play, but it takes the edge off our situation. We were tuned for battle.

"Van Loon will be asking questions." Silk worries about Katie. "He'd better not be too hard on that girl." Silk rarely displays anger, but this situation proves to her that she deals with madness. I do not believe Silk is angry at us, only angry at a world that resembles a funny farm.

"Blessings wear strange masques," Hal says. "Van Loon now lays aside his gun. He'll not be shooting." Hal's voice is troubled, and I must suppose he frets about Silk. Hal remains tense. This is the second time his adrenalin was up for battle, the second time that battle fades. He cannot stand idle much longer. Our man needs action.

"Get some sleep," I tell him. "It's about over."

"Would God that were true. We deal with demons." Hal takes his position of watchfulness. He will not sleep this night.

It is not yet very late, but tomorrow will be a greatly tiring day. I head for my lonely bed. When I rise it will be time to go into role.

XXIII

My trumpet hangs from my hand, and I wear my most handsome rags. I got shoes that flap soles to the beat of the street, and I got Roy Eldridge on my mind. Echoes of Storyville come callin', and I sing along with Louis and Oliver, then Velma scats before this horn. I've got that swing, that swingin' thing; and I feel Kid Ory's slide and Bigard's clarinet. I'm showboatin'. Yes.

I'm going to Mardi Gras, and today we're off the leash. Today I don't blat. I don't carry my bucket. Today's performance is a gift to sin city, and we'll have a little sip, and blow a little jazz across Jericho. Come climb on my beat, and tailgate your feet.

The bricks are drying, and clouds scatter like grace notes. Sun pretties up street art painted on fences and brick walls. Some of these artist cats are crazy. There's masterpieces out here, painted over worn-out bricks, with lots of squiggles and abstract stuff that's rightly musical. These street artists put in lots of hours, and it's just beautiful. Then some pop-eyed Barney Google comes with spray paint and spoils their scene.

The town lives along this street, but don't know créole beans about it. Executives zip past with attaché cases, like robins hopping on a lawn—"Hello, the name is Bob, Robert Robin, and insurance is my *game.*"

Jazz is workingman's music, and it takes workingmen to play it. These nabobs who hang around offices ain't got the staying power. They think this city is high-rise *everything,* but here on the street it's low-rise, gut-bucket. Jericho wakes to Mardi Gras, but Jericho don't *feel* it. Takes a lot of drum to wake this town, or, as they said in the district there in old, old New Orleans, "Let's hear the beat of them feet."

Take it the other way around, though, and you come up with a question. How can you have Mardi Gras when every day is Mardi Gras? Sin city is full of entertainments all the time. We got TV and pimps. We even got a little jazz.

I stand before a cash machine outside a bank, beating out "Mahogany Hall Stomp." My skin is dark as walnut juice, my hair is nicely kinky. Watery sunlight makes my brown hand glow beside the gold of this trumpet. Folks shake their heads and wonder what the hell? Then they remember this be Mardi Gras. Folks start smiling.

The day's still sanitary. Mounted cops on black horses stand around, and the horses got little leather baggies attached to their ass. A lot of *stuff* will be coming down, but horses get none of the action. Here and there a costume appears, clowns and jugglers, and already the mimes are out. A mime stands beside me and blows invisible clarinet. The cat is good, he makes it swing; but when coins don't drop he moves along. I got no blues in my shoes, not now, anyhow, and lay down "Maryland, My Maryland."

This role is growing wings. I feel close to this man, feel his notes like silver nails driven into the blank wall of a styleless world. I feel the drive of his blackness, and the beauty of his blackness. He's a top musician, and he's generous. Only second-raters feel the heat of competition. The great ones never put the slam on other musicians.

186

There's danger in this role, though. My man is pressed by music, so he tends to dawdle where music lives. I can't count on him to organize a thing, but that may not be a problem. I've hired two of the best grips to handle stage and props. My actors are pros, and have all the script they'll need.

I stand viewing the street. In this great city spires of churches spell out the world's religions. There are cathedrals here, and mosques. There are Buddhists, Muslims; while Indian totems rise in the parks. Today is Mardi Gras, and demons start to stream across the sky.

This role requires a lot. It took all morning to prepare. I must allow my music man his moods and directions as we swing into evening.

The street takes heat from my horn. I stand at a sidewalk café where the children sit digging a little sun. A smooth-hair honey, in a cute little wool suit, gives our man a dollar to blow the blues; but I *extend* a refund. Got no blues. Got no piano, either, but give her ten bucks' worth of barrelhouse.

Down the street a ways is a musician's bar across from union hall. Time for a little sip. I march in that direction, and think of James Petrillo. Oh, I got my card, but ain't a union man. Oh, no.

When folks built this bar they really *did*. Nice oak and plenty mirrors. Brass bar rail. Good Kentucky bourbon. Dear old Southland. Red whiskey smooth as duck feathers. Sipping whiskey. I stand at the bar while the bartender eyes my pretty rags. A couple of the boys sit at a back table and give our man the big hello. I wander their direction.

"You lookin' rather elegant," one says. His mouth is usually stuffed with a tenor. His belly pooches, and his shoulders are wide as Chicago. He's got Negro skin and Spanish hair. Got skinny Spanish lips, but still *does* that tenor. "You workin' or drinkin'?" says he.

"Yes, and yass," I tell him.

"Drinking and thinking." The other one's a Whitey; little skinny guy, and his eyes are starey. This kid don't look like he could even hold a horn, but just *pass* him a cornet. Bix was that-a-way. Bix just had *so* much inside. Too much, and I got to expect this child is the same.

"There's a direction you could drift," I tell them, "if you get lonesome. We putting on a little *performance*." I tell them where and when. They sort of dig it.

We drink and *con*verse about musicians. Who's working, who ain't. Our man on cornet got woman trouble, and ain't got work. His eyes are hurtful. We *know* the problem, and check for gigs in the local worksheet. Downright discouraging:

THRASH VOCALIST TO JOIN/FORM SERIOUS, ORIGINAL, SPEED METAL BAND, INTO TESTAMENT, EXODUS, MYRA-MAINZ.

"The times done passed me by," our sax man says. "Look at *this* shit."

YOU SUCK, WE SUCK, LET'S JAM. PLEASE, NO HM FAGGOTS, NO FRINGE, NO WOODSTOCK, NO SELF-PROCLAIMED HARD-CORES, NO BAKEHEADS, NO FUCKERS. WE NEED A DRUMMER AND 2ND GUITARIST. YOU'RE FUCKED UP AND SO ARE WE. LORDS, HANOI, SMACK.

This time of year the dark comes sooner than usual. Shadows get longer in the street. I ramble while there's still a little sun. Job sheet gives me a taste of the blues. The trumpet man is always the lead, the boss, but this trumpet's got no *coterie*. Got no sidemen. I ease in the direction of the homosexual bar, and blow a little Debussy. Bix got mixed with Debussy. Reckon all of us are searching, and tell ourselves we ain't.

Where do notes go? Do Bix's notes sail out there now, somewhere around the moon?

Is that a lonesome notion? I hate to see . . . that evenin' sun.
. . . A little girl stands blowing flute in front of her little hat. Hat lies
on the sidewalk. Brownskin girl from Juilliard, or some such place.
Negro skin and Indian hair, hair hanging to her waist. I blow a
question t'oard her. Are you feelin' lonesome? I run the line of
"Memphis Blues," and do she pick it up? Oh, yes.

Trumpet and a flute. Jazz don't care who plays it. If a man was
total crazy, he might-could play it on accordion. Trumpet and a
flute.

This child's a fine musician. She swings with the line, and sits
right on the beat. We start talking back and forth, with shadows
running longish. Lights flick here and there as signs come on. The
street is getting busy.

Our notes sing across the tops of cars, and go poking down alleys. They busy themselves around folks in costumes, folks dressed
like devils and alligators and dragons. Folks wearing clown suits
and tuxedos. A very-very dark man walks past, wearing a hat left
over from Saint Patrick's Day. Hat reads, "Kiss me, I'm Irish."

These notes ain't headed for the moon. They pry their way
through shadows, run rooftops, slide down gutters. These notes are
strokes of bluest blue lighting the faces and clothes of nuns and
harlots, Frenchie sailors, candymen and drunks. These notes got
eyes. They peer about the city. They're seeing everything.

Darkness clusters in the corners of her room as Katie Van Loon
stands before her mirror. Her costume is made from an old wedding dress bought at a thrift store. Stubby Dutch fingers have al-
tered the dress in a clumsy way, as Katie attempts to become a
princess. A tiara, made from an embroidery frame and decorated
with gold paper, keeps trying to slip from her head. She anchors it
in her hair. Her aspect is virginal.

The man who paid for the sweaters may come to see her. His
new sweater is hidden in a shopping bag beneath the front porch.
She doesn't want him to be mad at her. She was afraid he was dead
when his truck burned up.

Katie does not know, and would not believe it if she were told, that the man likes his killing best when he dresses his women beforehand. He takes pleasure from intruding into lives before he takes the lives away. All Katie knows is that the man will want his sweater.

At the Ramirez house men gather and dress as Elgin makes gentle sounds. Elgin wears a black robe of burlap, and a black hood encloses his face. Penitential eyes gleam from the shadows of the hood. Elgin whispers to robed men, then turns to Jorge Ramirez. Ten-foot lengths of logging chain lock around Ramirez' feet. They clank and trail in straight lines, and, although Jorge is physically strong from hard labor, chains drag at him and he can walk but slowly.

At The Sanctuary Silk lights candles and softly weeps. Silk is not a kid. She knows why she weeps. Silk is even smarter than her friends believe. Premonitions of tragedy wrap around her, but they come not from the hysteria attending age or religion. Silk knows that too much energy runs through this early evening. She understands that good and evil are not opposites. They are independent forces cruising the universe. Sometimes they collide. Silk watches young Hal, and it seems to her that he stands in a mantle of holy light. Such a vision would comfort most people, but Silk was once a nun.

Before the homosexual bar, workmen assemble a stage while a television crew unpacks. A news anchor stands beside her producer. The woman has an intelligent face and high forehead. Fatigue, that comes from years of accumulating words, seems a part of her charm. "My source is crazy as a loon," she says, "but he was big a few years ago. If we don't get what we want, we'll get some kind of story."

"It's goddamn faggy out tonight," the producer says. He holds a light rain jacket before him, as if protecting his crotch. Gaity swirls around him as costumed people dance in the street, or enter the bar.

Symptomatic Nerve Gas cruises through the growing crowd as he delivers his message in a command voice. He tells himself that everyone in this mess is nuts, and he is nutsiest of all because he knows better. At the same time, Silk and Hal and Elgin are too dumb to take care of themselves. Someone's got to do it. Symptomatic Nerve Gas cruises, but he stays near The Sanctuary.

Katie's father, Van Loon, tells himself he does not know what the hell is going on. His daughter keeps something from him, but she became hysterical when the black van burned. Van Loon suspects that one of those characters who hang out at the old church is responsible for the fire. He tells himself he would have had the police move them out long ago, except then some real tramps would move in. He reminds himself that the woman called Silk helped Ramirez.

Van Loon is not a bad man, only a man who tends his own fences. He slips into a light jacket as he stands in his bedroom. He hesitates, then steps to the closet, reaching back to the recesses of a high shelf. He brings out a pistol, stands looking at it as if puzzled. He is indecisive. Then, almost regretfully, he slips the pistol into his pocket.

A half mile from The Sanctuary, an XK-140 eases into a parking space, and a tall woman climbs out. She dresses in loose fatigues, like an aviatrix from the 1930s. Her hair hangs beneath a leather cap. Black ribbons entwine in her hair. They look like the snakes of a Medusa. Pockets of the fatigues are large. Weapons could fit in those pockets.

She moves rapidly, and puzzled men turn to watch her. There is something unsettling about the woman. She appears female in every way, but she walks like a male intent on important business.

Moist air from Puget Sound carries fog that is not much heavier than mist. Fog is pressed back by the heat of the city, and by the heads of thousands who cavort along the street. Fog hangs above a street preacher who hands out balloons, and above policemen on horseback. It touches burn scars on the face of an old wino named Tex who sits in the entryway of a pawnshop. Fog cannot muffle the hoots of bikers, but it may give comfort to expressionless Chinese who recoil before the jollity of the street where people in Fat Lady costumes, and Fat Man costumes, dance jiggly beside young girls. Fog cannot dampen the voices of a trumpet and a flute, as a walnut-colored man and a brownskin girl march like kissing cousins to the beat of "High Society."

XXIV

Time to *call* the children home. I stand on one corner of this stage blowin' hot as the multitudes assemble. Out there somewhere a tenor cranks up, and a cornet answers my horn. Flute rises like a kitten hopping on fences, and back of me some cat drums *it* on a garbage can lid. He's using chair rungs for sticks, like they did in old, old New Orleans. A gent hops up beside me, and it's a whole *second* before I dig his style. He's got no slide, he's got a voice. This man sound exactly like a trombone. He dances as he pushes his invisible slide and sings the trombone notes. Did he have freckles and bigger ears, we're seeing Trummy Young. He even sort of sound like Trummy.

We got a band. We got the Original Rain City Jazz Band. As the children come together we swing "If I Ever Cease to Love."

Streetlights and pink light shine on folks. This stage is fixed like a courtroom, or a gamble den. Big bench with chairs for judges, and a wheel of chance for spinning. Crazy. Crazy. I look out on a thousand costumes, donkey heads, Grecian robes, and that cat Felix. There's all kinda things out there. Mouse suits and fox suits, hep and hip. A little whiff of Mary Jane comes swirling, while juice-heads sing next to angels and trolls. Television cameras point, but that's no nevermind. All they catch is a dark-skinned trumpet man. Don't see no demons. Yet.

We're a long, long way from Beulah Land. There's some fright in this night, beneath all this light. Somethin' demonic.

I look far and away above the heads of the crowd. From the stage I can see quite a piece. Lots of frolic, but two blocks off folks ain't jumping. Can't hardly see what *occurs*, but it looks like some kinda parade heading t-woard us.

"Ladies and Gentlemens of Fog City," I holler. "From far-off Walla Walla, and at enormous expense—*yass*—we bringing you a little street theater—*yass*—by the world-famous Chester A. Arthur Mime Troupe—*yass*—straight from performances before the crowned heads of Europe." I turn back to the empty stage. "And here be your interlocutor for the evenin's entertainment. *Take* it, Mr. Bones." Me and the trombone man get off the stage and stand in front of it. Our band forms around us.

A gentleman hops on the stage, hands clasped over his head like a winning fighter, but he's dressed in a black suit like Simon Legree, or maybe a lawyer.

LAWYER: "I'm the persecuting attorney, ladies and gentlemen. We're going to have a trial. And here's our first judge."

A distinguished-looking man in black robes steps onto the stage. "I'm Judge Rompers. The Honorable Samuel J. Rompers, and I'm a white sonovabitch who knows his shit." Judge takes his seat at the bench.

LAWYER: "And here's our second judge."

A lean black man in black robes steps onto the stage. "Name of Moses," he says. "The *Right* Honorable Moses M. Moses." He takes his seat at the bench, then turns to the other judge. "Hey, white folks."

WHITE JUDGE TO LAWYER: "A jig judge?"

LAWYER: "They're taking over *everything*, your honor." Lawyer turns to the crowd. "And we got a lawyer for the defense."

A woman wearing suit jacket, and a skirt six inches above her knees, hops on the stage. She giggles. "My name is Wanda Wanta. I win most all my cases."

LAWYER: "By boffing with the judge."

WHITE JUDGE: "Yes."

BLACK JUDGE: "Oh, my, *yo.*"

LAWYER: "We got a defendent."

A pale young woman in long white gown steps onto the stage. Her makeup looks luminous. "I'm Jolene, and I'm dead. Why are you people messing with me? That don't seem right."

WHITE JUDGE: "You're not as dead as you're gonna be."

BLACK JUDGE: "She look pretty dead to me."

LAWYER: "And we got a plaintiff."

A man in black tights hops onto the stage. He wears a black mask. "I'm Acidophilus. I'm a demon." Points to defendant (aggrievedly). "Spent a lot of time and money killing that one."

DEFENSE LAWYER: "Objection."

BLACK JUDGE: "Sustained, sweets."

LAWYER: "And here's the star of our show—here's the brightest light in the firmament of the legal biz. Here's

*** Vanna ***"

An attractive young woman steps onto the stage. She wears a transparent gown over a transparent swimsuit. "I spin the wheel. That's what I do."

WHITE JUDGE (worriedly): "Don't get a titty caught in that thing, honey."

VANNA: "Been doing this for quite awhile, your honor."

LAWYER (looks down at the band): "Give us an introduction, Maestro."

I blow two bars of circus stuff, heralding stuff. Band picks it up, kicks a couple more bars, then tries to steal the show. I don't cut 'em off real quick. I'm checking the action.

There's something going on maybe a block and a half away where that parade is comin' from. I stand on the toes of my flappy-sole shoes and *revue* what I see. Television cameras are covering that stage like settin' hens. The newslady is smiling behind her hand, giggling at the awful jive. I cut the band off, but keep a sharp eye. From where we stand in pink light I can see Hal's blond hair like a whitespot on the top step of The Sanctuary. Pretty soon the court will call a witness to that stage. It will be time for me to chop-chop up there and identify the murderer. Meanwhile the play goes on.

ATTORNEY: "Defendant is charged with being dead, and with contributing to the deliquency of a demon."

DEFENSE ATTORNEY: "Move for dismissal. You can't try somebody who's dead."

WHITE JUDGE: "Shit, honey, we do it all the time."

BLACK JUDGE: " 'Cause that's when it's safest."

VANNA: "Anybody want me to spin this thing?"

BLACK JUDGE: "Which thing, sweets?"

WHITE JUDGE: "Hell, give it a whirl."

Clickety-click go the sound of the wheel. I look near in around the stage. Katie Van Loon stands close by, between a citizen in an elephant suit, and a scofflaw who looks like a pirate. Katie got stars in her eyes as she watches Vanna. Vanna might as well be naked, and Katie's thinkin' about that.

VANNA: "We got a winner for Acidophilus. A year's supply of Milk Duds."

DEMON (hops up and down): "I can't believe it. Oh, I *can* believe it. Oh, I *can't.*" (Hugs Vanna and cops a feel. Starts throwing Milk Duds to the audience.)

LAWYER (aggrieved): "I thought we were spinning a conviction."

BLACK JUDGE: "Got to do the trial, honk-head. Cain't convict without a trial."

WHITE JUDGE: "Enter the plea."

DEFENDANT: "I'm dead. There don't seem no way to get out of that."

DEFENSE ATTORNEY: "My client's a good Democrat, your honor."

I see a nose, oh Lord, and my hands begin to tremble. The murderer can take disguises, but can't hide that nose. Got to stay in role. The murderer has come to break up this play. The murderer is after me.

The murderer stands behind Katie Van Loon, and he's—she's—setting up some kind of deal. Katie nods and giggles. Murderer points to The Sanctuary, then to Cathedral Mansion, makes a joke. Katie laughs. From across the way Vandermeer's Great Dane woofs. Don't know what *occurs*, but this ain't supposed to happen. The murderer got black ribbons hanging in her hair, like a kicky Rastafarian. Behind the murderer stand three young girls, and one has a cardboard box. Don't know what's in the box.

DEFENDANT: "I wasn't contributing to anything, your honor. If you got a delinquent demon it ain't my problem."

BLACK JUDGE (to demon): "This here's a white girl?"

DEMON: "Half of my women are colored, your honor. Fair is fair."

BLACK JUDGE: "My *man!*" (Leans across bench and shakes demon's hand.) "What *inspires* you?"

DEMON: "None of these women are real, your honor. They're bimbos. When I kill 'em it makes them real. At least for a couple minutes."

DEFENSE ATTORNEY: "Objection."

WHITE JUDGE: "Put it in a sock, toots. This feller's got a plan. He's not a welfare bum."

Things are getting quiet up the street. I'm watching Katie, and she turns from the stage and kinda slides through the crowd. She's pointed toward The Sanctuary. The murderer backs away. The murderer raises her hand and makes a signal, but it's the sort of motion a man makes. Something is going wrong on stage. Something's trying to grab my actors' attention. One of the TV cameras swings ninety degrees, pointing up the street. A second camera swings. One camera stays on us.

WHITE JUDGE: "Everybody's guilty as hell. I'm gonna give you boys a summation."

The man is a fine actor. Now he rises and begins to drawl. He's putting down some Mark Twain–type jive, talkin' about the weather. He'll keep it up, and then he'll fade it when he finds a spot to bow out graceful. We've lost our audience as silence falls along the street.

This is all kind of *in*sane. The murderer is in the male personality, but he's disguised as a woman. I look up the street, then look back. Can't find the murderer. How can things move this fast when everything else is moving so slow?

All of a sudden we develop a hot spot. Over at Cathedral Mansion a bunch of bikers whoopie. Strings of firecrackers start to explode. Sounds like gang warfare, hundreds of little pistols. The crowd looks that-a-way, and from the roof of Cathedral Mansion bikers start setting off skyrockets. Skyrockets dash up past the bell-tower of The Sanctuary, exploding in hot little fires. Bikers shoot roman candles at the crowd, but the colored balls of fire burn out before they make it to the street.

The murderer has set this up. He wanted to bust up our play. Cops on horseback holler like crazy as they head toward Cathedral Mansion. Cops going to bust up *that* show. Horses clackety-clack on pavement, raising their high behinds to the crowd. I can't find the murderer. I struggle to stay in role. The third TV camera swings away from the stage. My actor has closed out the play.

* * *

Now flowers begin to fall on the stage, and on the heads of the band. These are mostly carnations, with stems trimmed short for easy throwing. Three young girls pull them from the cardboard box and toss them at us. The girls don't know why they're doing it, but they're having fun. Our murderer has set this up, oh Lord.

Flowers fall all around us. One bounces from my cheek. I want to scream, want to save the role; try to raise the trumpet to my mouth and can't. I'm coming out of role, another role murdered.

Flowers fall on the band and the flute player laughs and tries to catch them. She's a young woman, she's not afraid of flowers. The sax man tucks a carnation behind his ear. He's looking jolly.

I've made the worst mistake I've ever made. Nothing can be worse. I talked about the murderer, and called him a demon, but didn't believe it. In my heart I thought he was only a psychopath.

These flowers could be a lucky guess, an accident. I don't believe that, but as I struggle to get away from the flowers I tell myself that I want to believe it.

Flowers are the way he plans to silence me. If I react insanely, no one will pay attention to what I say. If I can control my reaction it's still possible to win. I look for a place to hide, and know that the best hiding place is in plain sight. I climb onto the empty stage, pretending that I'll blow this now-useless horn. It's a mistake, because I see what comes toward us. I'm immobile. Completely stopped.

It's all Elgin's show, and you can't explain poetry but you can tell about it. My mind runs the catalogs of information an actor knows from the many, many years of study. What we're seeing is not purely Spanish, and it's not purely Mexican. It's a divine combination and profane combination, and it's dark. Elgin brings hell and Good Friday into Mardi Gras.

In Tepoztlán, and other places in Mexico, people do not believe in fiery hells. Damn'ed spirits are condemned to walk the night while dragging chains. In Madrid they drag the chains on Good Friday, and carry the cross.

Jorge Ramirez heads the procession of penitents. He walks the cold pavement in bare feet scraped raw and bleeding. Heavy logging chains drag from beneath a black and hooded robe. Part of the blood comes from manacles holding chains to his ankles. The chains move slowly, slow as chilled snakes, their clanking voices small and dull against the street. Pink light falls across Jorge's hooded face, so the face is swallowed in the hood's dark shadow. On his back, and trailing, and rising above his head is a cross that is not only symbolic. This is a working cross made of four-by-six, at least nine feet long; long enough that, placed in the ground, it would stand sufficiently high.

Jorge Ramirez, father of Maria, doomed to walk this earth in chains. Jorge, who works at day labor for a dog's wage. This small man who the world has humbled from the day of his birth, leans tiredly forward beneath the weight of chains and wood. This man who fathers daughters for the world to kill, stepping in pain, a glory of pain. He has not even the honor of showing his face, only the hood which shadows him like a shroud. Weight bends him forward, like a tired swimmer up river. Penitence brings him not to heaven, but to the splendor of this street where even bikers cease to hoot. Pink light pinions him blackly against black pavement.

The crowd pushes back, gives way before him. People murmur, then silence each other. The voices of the chains mutter, and even the sky—where there should dwell the sounds of planes or sirens—even the sky stands silent.

Fog swirls above the procession which follows Jorge. Forty men in ranks of four lean into the weight of chains, although these are lighter chains. Forty cloaked figures with faces enfolded by hoods, stepping with bare feet against the fog-slick street. There are white feet beneath those robes, and black. There are Asian feet and Indian. The fathers—and at least some of them are fathers— lean against weight, although most of the weight lies in their souls. Each carries a smaller cross bearing the picture of a daughter. Old men, older men, young men. The procession moves in silence except as the lighter chains clatter.

The pictures of young women move past. Smiling girls. Laughing girls. Teeney's face floats in the fog. Her father's small frame bends with grief. Maria's face laughs through mist, from a cross carried by her uncle.

Girls who found their ways to the street, who did not find the way back. If guilt lies among these men, or some of them, it dulls now before this penitence. The pictures move past. Smiling girls. Laughing girls.

Elgin shuffles at the rear, his chains too heavy for an old man; but Elgin carries no cross. He carries a tall stake which holds a picture of the murderer. There are no words beneath the picture, no name. Here rises the great silence of poetry, the awful power of meaning that lives between words. The murderer's face rises above and behind the laughing faces of young women.

And then the clear voice of a horn rises, but this is not a dirge. Our cornet man, our man who feels pain like Bix once did, who is voiceless as Bix once was, raises his horn to "Swing Low, Sweet Chariot."

I stand confused and humbled. I thought when Jericho fell, it would fall to the voice of my horn; this horn that now hangs useless at my side. A TV camera swings toward our cornet man. I stand silent.

Elgin has trumped me, and trumped the murderer. The murderer came to intimidate me, kill me, and to break up the play. Now the murderer is identified. I failed, the murderer failed, and now Elgin walks in deadly danger of death by the murderer's knives. I've never had such courage. I've used my sacred art for hiding.

The band moves in behind the cornet as slow notes brush stripes of hope across the mist. Notes rise like spirits, and I do not know how a white cornet man can understand hot fields of southern cotton, or endless California fields. He does, though. The cornet is the voice of the voiceless, of men and women bent in stoop labor above crops. The voice is the sound of birth in shacks where wind pours through crevices, and it is the sound of the hoe striking dull through every daylight hour. Our man understands the street, the awful hunger behind jive, and the belly hunger of down-and-out.

I lay my horn on the stage, where, perhaps, some kid will find it; maybe experiment with it instead of going to a hockshop. Katie is nowhere to be seen. I can't find the murderer. The procession moves like black kites steady in a steady wind.

Across the way Silk stands beside Hal, and something bad must be happening. Silk grasps Hal's arm. She tugs at him, like an actress portraying flight. Hal seems to be shaking his head. He points to the crowd, out there where Symptomatic Nerve Gas lingers somewhere at the edge of the parade. Hal removes Silk's hand from his arm. He insists.

Now the flute joins the cornet, and its voice rises like the flight of white birds above the bowed heads of penitents. Feathers of music.

Then, and may this *not* be happening, Hal reaches over his shoulder and draws that sword. Silk descends the steps as she runs to find Symptomatic Nerve Gas. Hal's movements are smooth as running water. He carries the sword upright before him, the two-handed sword that could dismember elephants. He moves like the spirit of wind, not in the direction of the street, but into the inner recesses of The Sanctuary. The sword casts a thin line of pink light as Hal disappears into darkness.

The game is up. Our drama dashes to the finish line, but, oh, it was not supposed to end this way. Fear brings strength as I run. The crowd parts before me. Desperation carries me through the parade of penitents. My shoes flap as the voices of the cornet and flute sing hope and glory. The crowd ebbs like a small sea before my screams. People figure that the dark man who flies toward them is drugged out and crazed. They want nothing to do with it, and make passage. The Sanctuary looms high above me. My mind screams. My screams are answered by laughter from the belltower. Behind me penitents walk slow as winter's cold, but before me live the hot screams of hell. The steps to The Sanctuary seem high and impassable. It is possible to stumble up them amid demonic laughter that mixes above the musical voices of hope.

It must be the murderer. How did the murderer get inside The Sanctuary? We were boarded up. We were boarded. The only time we were all away from The Sanctuary was for a few minutes when the black van burned. He must have gotten in then, broken away boards for exit and entry. We've been tricked at every turn. Somehow the blame for this belongs with me.

I leap through the vestibule and into The Sanctuary. Candlelight rises in squelching darkness, so candles seem no more than markers; the lights of landing strips, or the nightlights along the halls of institutions. Shadows cluster in all niches, and darkness is a blanket overhead. Katie Van Loon begins to scream. Hal is in a standoff. Young Hal is stopped.

Horror has arrived from one quick flash of a knife—ghastly damage. Katie lies before the altar as the demon stands above her. Black ribbons hang like snakes in candlelight as Katie struggles to stand, then falls. Blood spreads across the long skirt of that white wedding gown. She is hamstrung behind one knee. Her face is flat with terror, her eyes crazed as the demon's knives hang like two judgments above her. Hal stands fixed.

"It's not a woman," I gasp. "Demons take any shape."

Hal is stopped in two ways. He fears Katie will be stabbed if he moves, but Hal is also a gentleman with a code. He would never strike a woman.

"That I ken. Get thee from hence," he tells me. His voice rings cold as the steel in his hands. "Our sorrow falls in this direction, yet Silk must not be harmed."

It's necessary to do something quick. Katie bleeds. The blood is not arterial, but it is profuse. I reach back into my memory. I have used roles, and somewhere among those roles must be a voice that will work. I'm not sure I've got the right voice, but it's worth a try. I switch into my pool hustler's voice. "You're done," I tell the demon. "We'll have cops in a few minutes. Give it up, bud."

The demon laughs. Its face changes. This is not the male personality, nor it is the female. From memory I recall such change. During a phone call, once, there was this change. The demon stands, long hair flowing, black ribbons flowing, the slight swell of rising breasts as it brings its knives high. One is a stiletto, the other a woods knife. The demon's mouth twists in scorn of all things sacred. Its hands are long-nailed, like small knives. Black crevices of shadow cluster around eyes glowing red as the eyes of a bear in firelight. Candles flicker and toss the shadows. The demon watches Hal, but looks past Hal toward me. I'm the one the demon wants, if it wants anyone.

And yet, that must not be true. This *thing* must want all of us. It must have planned to leave Katie's corpse before the altar; then it would flee. Now the game is changed, the demon's race is run, and it no longer cares. Katie screams, grabs at carved ornamentation on the altar, tries to pull herself erect. She is too weak with shock. Blood colors her shoes.

All I've managed to do is tell the demon that it has but little time. Another mistake, or maybe not. At least it breaks the deadlock. Now the demon steps away from Katie, as it begins to circle Hal.

"If ye be man or woman drop the knives. If ye be fiend from hell give battle." Hal's voice sounds keen as the edge of that sword.

The demon laughs. It points the stiletto toward Hal's eyes. It circles like a boxer, but actually seems dancing.

Given a battle between experts with blades, odds favor the fighter with the knives. All the fighter needs to do is get inside the sweep of that broadsword. A two-handed broadsword should be an awkward thing.

As it moves the demon screams, and no scream from the bell-tower ever carried such violence. This scream rises inhuman as the wail of medieval night. Twin sticking points of knives gleam in candlelight as the demon dances. The demon feints, tries to draw Hal in, tries to get him to commit a downward swing with the sword. Hal steps left, steps right, points the sword toward the demon's face. Hal looks clumsy. His movements are awkward. The demon laughs. We all believed Hal knew how to handle that blade. His white hair glows redly in candlelight. Katie lies silent. She is now unconscious.

The demon feints left, moves quickly right. The point of Hal's sword follows. The demon repeats the movements, setting up a pattern. The point of the sword follows. Hal backs up a step. He seems fearful and confused. The demon repeats the pattern, left, then swiftly right. The sword swings, a little too far. Hal nearly leaves an opening.

The demon repeats, but this time it is left, then right, then quickly left as the tip of the sword hangs too far to the demon's left. There is an opening. The demon spins, twisting into the gap, the woods knife low in the right hand; and a scream of triumph rises with the thrust. The sword drops, turns in a tight circle. The demon's scream layers like fog through darkness of The Sanctuary, a wail of victory that echoes, echoes . . . and then chokes in a stutter of disbelief.

The sword drops as the demon twists, then the sword rises faster than the strike of a cat. Hal was dissembling. The knife thrust continues, the demonic hand with the woods knife flying past Hal in a clear miss, Hal's movement so quick I do not understand what happens. The hand flies, tumbling, bumps against the top of a pew, then falls onto the seat of the pew. Fingers slowly loosen, unclasp, and the knife lies across the hand which trembles with tiny jerking movements as severed nerves stutter. Long nails are like dancing knives. I watch the hand, then realize what has happened, though it happened too fast to see.

Wails from the belltower. There are also voices from outside as men dash up the steps. One is Symptomatic Nerve Gas, and the other voice is Van Loon. The demon stands while arterial blood pumps. There is no fear or pain on the demon's face, only slight confusion that rapidly changes to hate. The creature is past sanity, past all redemption, and the stiletto in its left hand glistens. The demon dives toward Hal, a thrust toward the eyes.

The sword makes a little nipping movement, upward, a tiny strike, and the left hand falls, followed by the hot pulse of arterial blood; and it is now that the wail of the demon calls to wails from the belltower. The demon stands handless, waiting, and shock no longer protects against pain. Pain runs across the jerking body, still erect, heart still beating, pulsing blood. The mouth of the demon trembles, its eyes no longer red, but black in shadows. It falters. Confused. It makes a vague decision to flee. Blood lays a wet and heavy trail as the demon turns. It stumbles toward the basement.

"Handless then, it treads its way to hell. I wot well Satan will be pleased." Hal ignores the sounds of voices and running feet from the entry of The Sanctuary. He turns to Katie, who lies unconscious before the ornately carved altar. He leans over her, and with the sword begins cutting away cloth from the gown so he can bind her wound. I turn as a sense of doom feels its way through the darkness, what doom I do not know.

Running feet pound, as Van Loon and Symptomatic Nerve Gas try to get down the narrow aisle. They impede each other. Then, Symptomatic Nerve Gas grabs the corner of a pew. He launches himself, like a man emerging from a foxhole. A ball bat swings from his left hand. Van Loon stumbles. He falls, and bangs his head against the side of a pew. He becomes a rolling ball of anger and fright. Then he begins to rise dazed to his feet. Hal leans above Katie, cutting cloth from the skirt. There is not much cloth that remains unbloodied.

"Where the hell is he?" Symptomatic Nerve Gas raises the ball bat, searches the darkness for the demon. Blood lies before the altar, and it seems an infinity of blood. Pink light faintly illuminates stained-glass windows, and pink light falls through holes in those windows. Blood from Katie, blood from the demon; and the blood lies slick and black as the depths of history. Symptomatic Nerve Gas trembles. Too much blood runs in his memory, and now he stands momentarily stopped. He remembers the blood of women and children. The ball bat hovers in the air above Hal and Katie.

I turn toward the entry. Silk's running feet urge me back to her, back toward my love. She must be intercepted, must not see this. Silk must never know that such horror exists. As I turn I yell. It is not Silk who must be intercepted, but Van Loon.

Van Loon stands, still dazed. His face swells with desperation. He sees a man with a sword leaning over his daughter. Van Loon stands with pistol pointed, and from his stance Van Loon knows nothing about pistols; knows not even the rip and tearing that they do. I'm yelling, "No, no, no, no," as I dive, catching Van Loon around the ankles. An explosion rings above me as Van Loon topples. He tries to twist away, then falls heavily against a pew. His head makes a terrible smack against wood, the pistol drops from his hand, and he is out cold. I do not believe he is dead.

A quick, hard sob of disbelief brings me back to my feet. It is Silk who sobs. She hurries past as I rise.

Hal stands in candlelight, and in this Sanctuary such light was holy, once. In the first moment Hal seems unsure. Then gentleness, even a kind of love, forms about his mouth and eyes. The forest green jerkin darkens, as candles show blood staining and spreading across his breast. Hal trembles slightly, and candlelight gleams golden on his white hair. Then he places the tip of the sword between his feet. He shakes his head as if to clear it, grasps each side of the handle, and leans above the sword. The sword is a sturdy prop which momentarily sustains him. Hal looks like a young warrior of God from ancient days as he stands before the altar. He seems not a knight—although he seems that as well—but a sainted presence. Tears form in my eyes. Candles grow halos that dance about Hal's face.

And then his knees buckle, and he quietly falls. Only the sword makes noise as it clatters before him.

Silk arrives as he falls. She pushes Symptomatic Nerve Gas aside as she tries to catch Hal, then falls with him. Symptomatic Nerve Gas stumbles, kicks the demon's severed hand, and blinks muddily. He looks down at what he has kicked. Too much blood flows through his past, too many memories of explosions and the sharp smell of cordite. Symptomatic Nerve Gas sees the hand, then gropes his way to a pew and covers his eyes. He sits sobbing.

Sounds of several people come from the vestibule. The Sanctuary is invaded, first by demons, and now perhaps by anyone. Silk pulls Hal to her, raises his shoulders, and he lies in her arms; nestled in her arms. Silk's tears are as old as humanity, older than all the voices that have ever sounded through cathedrals. She sits in a great mixture of blood. She presses her cheek against Hal's face. Silk—who wanted to love small things only because there was too much despair in the world—becomes eternal art, rendered not in paint or marble, but in loss and blood.

Silk motions us away as Hal's breath shortens. His lips lie close to her ear. Hal whispers, whispers, and we do not hear his dying words; although we seem to understand a couple of them, and those perhaps only an ancient echo. "My lady."

Portable lights bloom in the entry to The Sanctuary as the TV flack gives her rapid orders.

XXV
CHORUS

I am a watcher among shadows. Far below in the street police pass harmless by, and instructions for the tax-return forms list no occupation called "watcher among shadows." A few people believe me deranged. Most neither know of me or care. I am in this world, but outside of it. I am of this world, but barely.

Police arrested all of us, retaining the unfortunate Van Loon on charges of second-degree homicide. Police listened to Symptomatic Nerve Gas as he spoke of the retreat from P'yŏngyang —how blood soaked the snow, and how torn bodies froze beneath the hot breath of machine guns. The police sent him to the VA's insane asylum. The street lies emptied of that command voice.

Because of her great grief, Silk was released as an inconvenience. She was mute beneath the weight of that grief, as if by silence she could keep despair from entering the world. I am told she now lives—in silence—in the attic of a Yankee's garage; because this, her new nunnery, failed her. Belov'ed Silk. Beloved.

I was released because I acted a role of being normal. It was my last willing role. I was at least that skilled. So skilled in fact, and so much accustomed to being so many selves, that I could not touch my own grief, only the grief of the role.

Hal's funeral should have been majestic, for I was willing to pay; but it was doubtless secretive and quiet. Hal's family in Virginia, who despised his living presence, found that it wanted his corpse. Dear Hal was shipped.

Katie Van Loon will live, but what a wounded life. When her father goes to prison she will visit him on crutches. At the Ramirez house, each night, the blue glow of television illuminates the windows, and in the early mornings Jorge trudges slow and silent to the labor pool.

And Elgin, gentle soul. He now lives beside an old, old woman, and perhaps they talk of olden days when the world held absolutes. I sometimes see Elgin passing in the rain-washed street. From this great height of the belltower I watch him sniffing through mist while uttering poems. He wends his tender way.

The demon was found at the foot of the steps in the basement, pale as the dead lime on which it lay; and I am told it seemed curiously melted, as if trying to enter the very foundations of this broken church. It was cremated, a fit rebirth into fire and smoke. I trust the severed hands went with it.

And the drama, itself? The fatal flaw rose because Hal and Van Loon were moral men cast to walk on a modern stage. They foolishly believed that men should protect children.

I sit in this belltower amid voices of rain and slamming wind. Bikers hoot from Cathedral Mansion, and pink light from the homosexual bar surrounds, like cotton candy, the gowns of those who enter. An occasional boombox rises into mist, pulsing with horror lying in the backs of young minds—horns must always play, and there must be jive, jive, jive—because (the horror says)—if the music ever stops you will find, young woman, young man, that none of us are home. You will find us trapped in the present; for horror rises not only from history, but from history denied.

The only voices here are wind and rain. There are no mumbles or chortles or shrieks. Yet, I think of demons. I think of the demon who is defeated, but think mostly about those demons that once screamed from this belltower. They were demons of past and present and future. In other days I wondered how long they had dwelt here. Now I understand when they arrived. There were no demons here before *I* came. Isaiah 59:14: "... for truth is fallen in the street, and equity cannot enter."

But the demons are in the street, if truth is not. The demons blow like black kites along the street.

And I nurture the sacred flame of art, but fail. The flame is little more than a dying ember. I understand how our demon was able to identify me so easily, attack so directly. The flame of my art burned bright, but I burned only with power and control. As an actor I forgot reverence. The street is filled with talk. Any number of people may have known who I was, but none would have known had I listened with the reverence my art deserves.

From some role, at some time, rises the memory of a story someone told, and which I now understand. It was about a monk who spent twenty years learning to walk on water, when, for a few cents, he could be carried across the river on a ferry.

How, then, could I ever offer blame? It was mostly I who failed. Mine is the final and fading voice. And yet, sometimes, I wonder if there is not more to it. Perhaps I will stand in this belltower and push these bells. This great boss bell will toll, like the mourning voice above a fallen city.

They, my friends, walked among us. We were people of the street. We accomplished naught but a great failure, though at least we tried. We were your lesser creatures, the poor, the awkward, the scorned, the mad, and the ungainly. Yet, in my fancy, I sometimes suppose that we were the last line of resistance in a world no longer able to know that resistance is necessary. Even the least of us were walls and bulwarks. Now we are failed and fallen, the walls are crumbled, ruin surrounds; and Jericho stands defenseless in the rain.